THE BIKER'S GIRL

A BAD BOY AND VIRGIN ROMANCE

LILY DIAMOND

HOT AND STEAMY ROMANCE

CONTENTS

Sign Up to Receive Free Books	1
Blurb	3
1. Chapter One	5
2. Chapter Two	12
3. Chapter Three	21
4. Chapter Four	28
5. Chapter Five	35
6. Chapter Six	40
7. Chapter Seven	47
8. Chapter Eight	59
Sign Up to Receive Free Books	73
Preview of The Hunter's Treasure	75
Chapter One	77
Chapter Two	85
Other Books By This Author	93

Made in "The United States" by:

Lily Diamond

© Copyright 2020 – Lily Diamond

ISBN:978-1-64808-082-1

ALL RIGHTS RESERVED. No part of this publication may be reproduced or transmitted in any form whatsoever, electronic, or mechanical, including photocopying, recording, or by any informational storage or retrieval system without express written, dated and signed permission from the author

❀ Created with Vellum

SIGN UP TO RECEIVE FREE BOOKS

Sign Up to Receive Free E-Books and Audiobook Codes.

Would you like to read **The Unexpected Nanny, Dirty Little Virgin** and **other romance books** for **free**?

You can sign up to receive these free e-books and audiobooks by typing this link into your browser:

https://www.steamyromance.info/free-books-and-audiobooks-hot-and-steamy/

Or this one:

. . .

HTTPS://WWW.STEAMYROMANCE.INFO/THE-UNEXPECTED-NANNY-FREE/

BLURB

Kitty

When I bought up the large piece of land beside a biker gang's home base, I was only thinking about getting a big enough space to open my animal shelter, Second Chance. Lucky for me the biker gang's full of a harmless bunch of teddy bears—especially when it comes to their dogs. If it weren't for the dogs, I might never have met Jake, the leader of the gang.

I've always had a good relationship with the guys, but I wouldn't mind a little something more from Jake—I haven't been able to stop thinking about him since the moment I met him. But he's never made a move in all this time, and I'm so inexperienced I wouldn't even know where to start on my own.

When an early cold snap threatens autumn litters of kittens throughout the area, I'm left scrambling to distribute insulated nesting shelters and rescue mama cats and their babies all over the area. I need help—and I know just where to get it.

The best part of this plan of mine is that I get to spend the next few weeks riding around from town to town spending time with Jake—who can make my toes curl with just a smile.

Jake

Now and again in my life, I run into a woman so pure and sweet that I just want to get her a little dirty—in all the ways she likes. That's what I think every time I look at sweet, thick little Kitty, who runs the animal shelter next door and keeps my dad's dogs healthy. I would love to make her smile—and scream. I'd even let her leave me with plenty of claw marks. But sweet little Kitty's so shy I'm still trying to figure out how to hit her up without scaring her off.

Now we've got the cutest rescue mission in the damn world on tap for the holidays, and the guys are having as much fun with it as I am. And the more Kitty warms up to me, the closer I get to what I really want for Christmas—her.

1
CHAPTER ONE

Kitty

It's close to midnight when I make my way up the steps to the Martin farmhouse's pillared, wraparound porch. I'm bundled up against the unseasonable cold; the nights have started dipping below freezing already and it's only November. It worries me—for a lot of reasons. But right now those worries are far from my mind, and I'm trying not to laugh as I approach the door.

I knock on the door and then glance around, smiling. My neighbor down the road has six acres in a long, tree-edged strip that runs back up into the hills. She's a military widow from New York City who decided to retire to the countryside, only to discover that we have our own challenges out here.

Mrs. Annabeth Martin is the kind of sweet old Christian lady who would give you the clothes off her back if she wasn't worried about modesty. She's easily scandalized, tends to pass judgment on people quickly, and is a strange mix of paranoid and naive. I try to be a good neighbor to her, but I always hide the pot and booze before she comes over.

My breath steams past my scarf as I wait for the shuffling footsteps that have started up on the other side of the door. I busy myself by looking around and hoping that I'm wrong about what I suspect I'm going to see when I get inside. The chuckle that sneaks out of me is half ironic.

Annabeth called me apologetically about a friendly stray dog she took in tonight, who turned out to be destructive and not at all housebroken. Since I'm the local vet and run a private animal shelter, I'm the only person in fifty miles that she could turn to. So I only grumbled a little on the way over.

She has two sons who come up from the city on weekends to help look after things, but the land's still looking pretty scruffy. No one has raked the black walnuts off the drive in weeks. The green rinds with their black innards have been torn open by squirrels and left scattered everywhere. The front lawn is adrift with dead leaves.

I turn back to the door as the footsteps get closer and hear the bolt clack as it's thrown. The inner door opens partway, and through the storm door, I see a puffy-haired Annabeth in a fluffy pink robe and big gold cross necklace. She beams as she sees me and hurriedly lets me in. "Come in, dear, come in. He's right in here. Watch your step."

She has spread out newspaper on the floor and I pick my way down the hall as it rustles underfoot. "So where did you find this dog?"

She leads me down her hallway into the kitchen, stopping by the closed door. "Well, he's been coming around begging since the late summer. He doesn't have a collar, so I thought maybe I could win him over and see if he wanted to become my new dog.

"It got so cold tonight that when he cried at the door I let him come running in to warm up, and he seems to want to stay. But he's really a handful. Eats a lot, tries to break into the cabinets, jumps up on the table, pees where he pleases, chews things...it's like he's never lived with a family at all! Not to mention that Mittens is terrified of him."

Oh boy. I am now eighty percent certain about what—and *who*—is hanging out in Annabeth's kitchen. Apparently nobody warned her about one of our neighborhood...characters. "All right, well, let's take a look at him and see what we're dealing with."

The musky smell of something a lot stronger than dog urine hits me as I walk into the kitchen, and I'm careful to watch my step. The culprit, looking fat and very proud of himself, is sitting on the breakfast nook table panting and grinning. I fold my arms and scowl at him, though I can barely keep from laughing.

"Um, Annabeth, sweetie?" I say as the beast on the table squints happily and chuffs at me. "That's...not a dog."

"What do you mean he's not a dog? Isn't he one of those African dogs that don't bark?" She sounds genuinely baffled.

"No, I'm sorry. You see, this is Randy. And he's definitely not a Basenji." I eye Randy as he gives me a saucy look and then starts wagging his tail exactly like a damn dog. No idea where he learned that trick, but it—along with his relative friendliness toward humans—apparently got his paw in the door over here.

"Well, what is he then? He plays, he doesn't bite us, he loves the food we give him..." Poor Annabeth is looking at me like I have sprouted another head.

I sigh. "Annabeth, I'm gonna suggest that you open the back door and let him out. I'm sure he'd be happy to winter with you and have you feed him. And no, he's not gonna bite you, at least not until he's on the couch and you want him to move, or he gets too excited while you're playing."

"But it's so cold! Will he be okay?"

I'm dying here. I'm literally leaving my body as we speak. I shoot a glare at Randy and swear he's laughing at me. "He'll be fine, I promise. He'll catch up with his pack and they'll winter down in the foothills."

My neighbor goes very still. Randy is now licking loudly at his balls. She looks over at him, and hesitantly asks, "Pack...?"

"Randy is a coyote, Annabeth. A spoiled, lazy, sneaky little poop of a coyote who has discovered that if he acts like a cute doggie humans will feed him." I eye Randy up and down, seeing that he's at least five pounds overweight and has a thick, glossy winter pelt. *It's a pretty damn good ploy, actually.*

Randy just grins at me and goes back to licking his balls.

"A coyote?" She stares in amazement. "But he's so friendly!"

"Yeah he is. Humans have food and have a huge soft spot for cute and friendly mammals, and he's figured that out. But look, Annabeth, even if he has discovered humans are easy marks, Randy's a wild animal. He will use your entire house as a toilet, and he will eat your cat."

"Oh no, not Mittens!" She covers her mouth with her hands, eyes wide with horror. I nod gravely, satisfied that she'll think twice before taking in any more "homeless dogs." *Good thing, too, because next time I'll probably come in here to see her new pet has antlers.* Annabeth really is a city girl through and through.

I arch an eyebrow at Randy, who chuffs again and wags his tail. "Forget it, man, nobody here's buying it anymore."

His tail lowers and he yaps at me in irritation, but there's still an edge of smugness to it. *Shithead. Cute, though.*

I'm on my way back to my truck a few minutes later, having calmed my embarrassed neighbor and left her with a bottle of enzyme cleaner. Randy is sitting on the hood of my truck when I reach it, panting and grinning at me. "Fattening up for winter on the old lady's dime, huh? You big mooch."

I can hear the high howls of the other coyotes echoing along the upper slopes. They've caught his scent, and are probably wondering where he was all night. I keep clear of biting range as

I walk around to the driver's side door. "Go on already; go find your pack. They're gonna be pissed you didn't share all your snacks."

He sneezes, then jumps off as I open the door. But instead of running off, his ears prick up suddenly and he looks down the road. I frown and turn on my headlights—just in time to see a feral cat scramble across the road maybe thirty yards away, with a dead rat in her jaws. Her belly hangs loose enough to flap; she's still nursing.

"Damn it." Another late litter. Normally I wouldn't have to worry too much, as local autumn kittens would typically be weaned and have a fighting chance by the time things started freezing over. Not to mention I'd normally have three more weeks to put together the insulated shelters I distribute around the area for the strays every year.

This time, though, there's been no such luck. And as I grab my flashlight and start tracking the feral through the woods, I feel my worry growing.

I'm the shy type. Most of my friends growing up had four legs, and that's still the case now. That's why I got my veterinary degree, why I sunk so much of my inheritance into the private shelter, and why I get pretty upset at the thought of frozen kittens.

I take photos as I go so I can find the cat's nesting spot again once I return with supplies. Finally, I spot the kitty climbing up a dead tree, disappearing into a big hollow about ten feet up. She's picked a good spot. The trunk's thick enough to insulate and protect her babies.

But there are a lot of abandoned and feral cats out here who either won't be as used to the outdoors, or who won't be as lucky in finding a good spot.

Deciding to bring some food and insulating bedding scraps for queen kitty tomorrow, I take a photo of the tree and then turn to go home. *This is a problem that I am going to need some serious help with it. Finding feral litters, sheltering and feeding those we can't relocate to my shelter, distributing the shelter boxes—and doing it all in under a week. Covering miles of road and over a hundred acres.*

My heart sinks. Normally I can get all this done with no problem; my work hours are low even with the shelter to run and the veterinary needs of the valley to take care of. But with my normal workload, the upcoming holidays, the kittens and socialized ex-ferals already in the shelter, and with freezing temperatures arriving three weeks early...

Maybe I can hire some emergency help. It's not like I don't have the cash. People around here don't know that I'm working not because I have to, but because I love what I do. I actually inherited more money than I know what to do with, but I just don't feel right not contributing to my community. Call it my Yankee work ethic.

As I'm driving up the road, I see the coyotes flood across the lane behind me, with Randy's fat butt leading the way. *Nice to see he's back with his family, but they need to go back up their hillside now.* There's another reason to fear for the cats and their kittens —the cold is driving the coyotes downhill too damned soon.

Yeah. I have to fix this.

My house is just up the road. I only drove my truck because it has the big kennel in the back and my dog-catching gear. But I'm not going home yet. I pass the small stone farmhouse and the sprawling barn beyond it, which houses the clinic and shelter. I drive right past my own driveway, headed for my neighbors down the hill on the other side.

The Ravens will still be up. They don't roll up their welcome mat until three. Jake and the guys owe me and I'm sure they wouldn't say no to making some extra cash.

Annabeth would freak out if she knew I was going to the

local biker gang—and resident pot growers—for help. She has this image in her head of what it means to be a biker, and she can't shake the idea that they're all dangerous men, instead of the tough but friendly guys they actually are. But they have never caused me problems, and since I'm the one they go to when their dogs get sick or have puppies, we have a pretty good relationship.

I hope it's good enough. There's an acre-wide strip of trees acting as a buffer between their land and mine, which is home to a lot of wildlife. Beyond it, their high hedges mask their property from the road, but I can see the glow of the house lights through them now that the branches are bare for winter.

My stomach flutters a little as I pull into their gravel driveway and the dusty lot beyond. *I hope Jake is home.*

Big Jake Steele is half the reason I make excuses to come visit. He's the hottest man I have ever seen in my life. Huge, burly—a wild man in leathers with shaggy black hair and a brutally handsome face with intense green eyes. He has a gravelly voice that turns into a slightly awkward purr when he is trying to be less intimidating, and the way his ass looks in his jeans makes it impossible not to stare.

Of course, I've never done a thing about it. But a girl can look...and a girl can dream.

I see his huge shape fill the doorway of the house as I park my truck, and my stomach flutters even harder—but I smile even more.

2
CHAPTER TWO

Jake

I'm on the couch polishing off my second beer and third coffee when my right-hand man, Morrie, comes in and tells me that Kitty is pulling into the parking lot. A smile breaks over my face; some of my exhaustion lifting off of me like a weight. "I'll go meet her. You guys keep feeding the dogs."

Dad has been having a rough night tonight. Nightmares. I took care of him until he felt well enough to want privacy, leaving him with two of the dogs and his bong. But it wore me out, and I was feeling pretty down, right up to the moment I heard Kitty was here.

Some of us come back from our time as soldiers with little scars, and some with big ones. Some on them are on the outside for everyone to see, but some, like my dad's, are mostly within. I got my Purple Heart for taking IED shrapnel, and have some scars on my leg and a little limp. My dad never feels safe, and screams himself awake sometimes.

The open road, our club, the pot we grow and smoke, the friends we make on the road and off, and each other—that's what we have to heal us. It works pretty well—that, and Dad's dogs.

I THROW on my jacket on the way out the door, and look out to see Kitty's truck headlights splashed across my front yard. She cuts them off and gets out, then heads for me, waving. I grin and raise a hand. "Evening!"

"HI THERE!" she calls up, and I try to fight my smile down, but the sight of her warms me. She's small, sweet-faced and very curvy, with a dynamite rack that even layers of clothing can't hide. She's got fluffy, curly hair the color of honey, eyes nearly the exact same shade, and a smile that's contagious.

IT'S PRETTY rare for me to meet someone that I want to hang out with all the time, cuddle silly, and fuck unconscious, all at the same time. Usually I just want to do one or two of the three when I meet a lady, but Kitty is special.

TOO BAD THAT if I proposed the sex part, I'd probably scare her off. She's sweet, shy, and tiny. I'm roughly the size of a truck, hung to match, and keep company with ex-convicts. I know she knows I would never hurt her, but the logistics alone would take some work to overcome.

I HATE BEING STUCK JUST WATCHING and wanting, but the fact that she's an awesome friend eases that frustration a bit. She gets along with everyone, we trade favors all the time, and my Dad loves her because she takes care of his dogs for him. But lately, I can't even finish with a woman unless I'm thinking about Kitty.

SHE SMILES UP AT ME, and it warms me on this cold night, even as I stand in front of her with my jacket open. "Hey, do you have a few minutes, or is this a bad time?"

"NO WORRIES, sweetheart. C'mon up, I've got a beer with your name on it." I step back, holding the door open for her as she bounces up the stairs. Immediately, happy barking starts up in the back of the house, and the whole pack scrambles toward the door at once. They know her and love her.

SOME WOMEN BECOME crazy cat ladies. My Dad calls himself a crazy dog guy. We laugh over it. But these rescue dogs—mostly pit bulls we saved from a fighting ring—give Dad a reason to get out of bed when he's having a rough time.

I DO whatever it takes to help him. The crash that disabled him and left me in charge of the bike club also made his PTSD worse. So, early last year, when he told me being around dogs helped his mood, we went looking for a puppy for him.

NOW THE COMPOUND HAS SEVEN. Four brindle and white Pits, a Rottie, a Husky-Tibetan mastiff mix named Chewbacca, and Laughing Boy, a coyote-dog hybrid whose dad, Randy, keeps visiting the neighborhood. They crowd around us, their tails wagging uncontrollably, as I lead Kitty inside.

"HI BOYS! HI MAGGIE!" Her voice is bright as they press in to get their hugs. I kind of wish I could line up with them and get a hug too.

IT REALLY IS a bunch of guys in this household; even the dogs. The whole crew is a sausage fest except for Maggie Grue, the oldest pit bull and mother to the others. Just sorta worked out that way.

KITTY DISAPPEARS HALFWAY into Chewbacca's russet fur as she hugs him, and he pants happily. *Goddamn, she's adorable. And her nice, round ass looks great in those jeans, too.*

LIKE ME, she likes to wind down with a coffee and a beer in each hand on cold nights. I pour her a mug and pull a longneck out of the fridge, and then come back into the living room to find her on one of the big, blanket-covered couches that line the room. Chewie has his head in her lap and she's already got a grooming brush in her hand.

. . .

"So, what can I do for you, sweetheart?" I ask as I flop onto the couch kitty-corner to hers. Two of the pits, Bo and Maggie, hop onto the couch next to me, and the others settle around our feet.

"I need your help—you and the guys. You know cold season has come early. That's big trouble for the local feral cats, and I have to prepare for winter three weeks early—and as fast as possible." Her face is serious as she works on the endless task of combing out Chewie's fur.

"Yeah, I noticed the coyotes are passing through the neighborhood early. The cold's driving all their prey downhill." I frown as I set her drinks on the coffee table in front of her and set the bottle of chocolate syrup within reach. "You seen Randy around?"

She snorts and reaches for the coffee first, setting aside the brush for a bit. She squirts syrup into her mug and stirs it as she talks. "Yeah. He's fine. He conned Annabeth into thinking he was a stray dog. She's been feeding him on her porch for weeks on top of his hunting with his pack. He looks like a sausage in a fur coat now."

I let out a bark of laughter, imagining it. That damn coyote is hilarious, but he's also a menace. If he can't eat your pet or livestock then he tries to eat their food, and when he's done with their food he tries to mate with them.

THE RESULT IS a local coydog problem that gave the little fucker his name, and led to Kitty offering free spay-neuter procedures for local pets. Laffy, who knows the word "Randy," keeps pricking up his ears as we talk. He was part of a half-German Shepherd litter of six.

KITTY TAKES an experimental sip of her makeshift mocha, and then a larger swallow. "The last few years, even with the spay and release program for the feral cats, we've had at least ten litters every autumn in the woods around here. A few of the queens will be smart in their choice of nests and will just need some help with food, but some will need to be completely relocated."

I NOD, frowning a little. It's a busy time for us; we've just got the autumn pot crop in and the whole thing is drying under the greenhouse tents. But I know I can't say no to her. Besides, if enough of the boys help out, we can handle the whole mess in a few days.

AND AFTER THAT she'll need help socializing kittens, which is hardly work at all.

"TEN LITTERS. And you've got room for them?" I lift an eyebrow. I don't know how she gets as much done in that shelter as she does—she must have either a pile of money I don't know about, or some kind of magic. She has a website, volunteers, people doing adoption days for her in cities and towns up and down the coast...and she just expanded her facilities again last year.

"Oh yeah, unless it's like ten litters of twelve or something. Then I might have a problem." She gives a little nervous laugh. Chewie whines at her, desperate to regain her attention, and she goes back to brushing him.

"I know I can get some of the guys to help out. We have to have at least four of us dealing with the curing process, but that leaves six guys to help you out."

"Seven," I heard my Dad's voice in the doorway, sounding tired but determined.

We look up to see him walking in with his cane, his grizzled face looking calm but focused. Dad and I resemble each other so closely that I pretty much know what I'm going to look like in about twenty-five years. Little grayer, little jowlier. Only the cane gives him any real appearance of being old.

"So what's going on?" he asks, limping over and plopping into his overstuffed chair across from the couch I'm perched on. He has his bong in his grip, and loads it from an Altoids tin while he listens to her explanation.

"Kitten season," she starts, and goes back over what she told me. He nods along, then takes a long hit and holds it before passing her the bong. She hesitates before taking a hit. "Annabeth would be shocked to see me smoking like this."

"Annabeth shocks too easily. This would help her plenty with her arthritis, and besides, it's been legal for years now," I say, noticing Dad shoot me a look to tell me to shut up about the old church lady. He's got a soft spot in his head for war widows, and it's not like Annabeth isn't a nice person.

But the truth is she's called the police on us twenty times in just the last year, and all for bullshit reasons. Guns we don't own, drugs we don't run, "suspicious people," noise complaints about our motorcycles in the middle of the afternoon. The cops are sick of her, but they can't really explain to their boss why the local (wealthy) innocent war widow keeps calling in a panic if nothing is going on.

"She does shock too easily, and she prejudges people. But I can manage her. I'll just get permission to search her acres myself. She owes me a favor now." She shoots my dad a placating look, and he nods with a faint smile.

"Anyway, point is, you'll have plenty of help," I'm confident in promising. "When will you need us?"

She flashes me that heart-warming smile again, eyes full of relief. "Mid-afternoon tomorrow would be great, or the next day if you have trouble pulling things together on time."

. . .

I NOD and revel in that smile, and in how she's looking at me. It makes a guy a little too hopeful. But I'll manage. I always do. "We'll be there tomorrow. No sweat. Now how about you pass me that bong and we'll make plans."

3

CHAPTER THREE

Kitty

The next day, the weather is a little warmer but the freeze has already taken its toll. Plants are withering and sagging, their colors going dull as they transform from living things to standing mulch. My heart sinks as I load up my truck with a mix of traps, insulated shelters, bedding scraps and food. The sight of the mess reminds me again of how little time we have.

I know the ecosystem around here pretty well. I'm not a full-fledged naturalist, but since I'm looking for lost and feral animals in the near wilderness, I decided to educate myself long ago. That, plus experience, has taught me that once the cold sets in enough for the plants to wither, the prey animals dig in or migrate. That meant three less weeks for the feral mothers to fatten for winter and wean their kits to do the same.

It also means that the other predators will be hungrier. Coyote packs eat cats, and certainly they eat kittens. A bear stuffing its face for hibernation will be under even more pressure now and will—if hungry enough—eat the cats, the kittens, and even the coyotes. In late fall and early winter, nature around here truly turns red in tooth and claw.

And then, everything freezes.

I'm just glad that Jake and the guys are going to help me. I need it so badly. And the cats do too, though of course, no cat ever would admit they needed some human's help, if they could admit anything at all.

Once everything is loaded up, I tarp and tie the whole stack against the rain that's threatening, and slip inside to start up the truck and get on the radio that the guys use to communicate. The moment I turn it on I hear the Ravens chattering on their helmet mics. "Hey, guys, this is Kitty signing on."

"Hey, sweetheart," purrs Jake, his voice in my ear making my toes curl so hard inside my boots that they crack. "So, we're parceling out the seven plots of land you pointed out, while you search yours and the Church Lady's."

"Watch that, kid," Jake's dad grumbles, and I fight back a laugh. He has a crush on Annabeth. I, for one, think they would make a great couple. They're about the same age, he's a vet, and she already knows about living with someone with PTSD. But she's the one who mistakes coyotes for dogs, and war vets for criminals. I'm not sure how we can get her past that.

It's a cute idea to contemplate, though. But if I'm thinking about improbable acts of Cupid...well. I'd rather start with me and Jake, even if that is a little selfish.

He's wonderful, though. I don't care that he and the guys were selling weed well before it was legal, or that they sometimes get into bar brawls. They're good people. He's a good person. And sometimes, when he looks at me...I forget for a little while that I'm shy and have the sexual history of the average nun.

Sometimes, I wish I'd end my nights crushed under him, feeling things I've never felt before while he groans in my ear.

I shake myself out of it after a few dreamy moments. "We're parceling them out, yeah, but we'll have to do them two at a time. We'll sweep northward along the road from town all the way up to the winter snow line. The cats won't go up above there; that's bear territory."

It gets easier to give out instructions as I go; the words detach from my throat and some of my shyness dissipates. "Each team will do a plot on opposite sides of the road. We'll skip over my land and Annabeth's and continue up the road on the other side once we get there. If you find cats, you mark the spot and call me there. I'll check it out and figure out how to proceed from there."

Ferals don't go far from the road. If they ever lived with humans then they like to stick by us. If they don't, road-kill and the rats, mice, and squirrels that our gardens attract are usually the cats' main prey.

Early in my rescues I would hike miles away from the road searching, but I never saw any signs of cats. I'd only ever find a lost dog or two, some curious bears, and Randy, who would follow me for miles for treats and attention, even though he'd only get his way sometimes. So now I concentrate on looking closer to civilization.

"How mean are these cats gonna be?" Jake asks, and I sigh, sitting back and thinking about it.

"It really depends. No queen cat is going to like strangers around her kittens. But if she was dumped out here after she got pregnant she should be pretty desperate to get indoors, and will trust humans more. If she was born out here, she'll be wary at best, and fight like the devil to protect her kittens."

I'm not kidding. I have scars from desperate queens who only figured out days later, once they and their kittens were well-fed, warm and safe, that I never meant them harm. "Let's just say that it's good that all you guys like wearing leather anyway."

The guys laugh and make a few rowdy comments about

dangerous pussy. I laugh too. I'm not very good at being a lady, and I don't ever bother around them because that's not what they expect. It's not even what they're comfortable with. I'll just have to dial it back when I talk to Annabeth about searching her land; raunchiness upsets her.

Everything upsets her. I wish that I could find a way to get through to her about how unnecessary that all is, but she lives in a very black and white world. Sometimes I worry that I'll make one single misstep, she'll overreact, and she'll start calling the police to my house as well. But then things like the mishap with Randy will happen, and I'm reminded that she's mostly just a slightly dotty but sweet old woman.

While I wait for the first call to come in, I prep another of the cat shelters. They are wooden boxes that are roughly the size of a plastic tote that I've waterproofed, lined with insulation, and put in smallish, high entrances. The design sheds snow and rain and is tough enough to discourage predators. It has bolts screwed into it for anchoring the shelter, either on the ground or in the crotch of a well developed tree. I stuff several handfuls of straw into it for even more insulation.

The wooden shelters are popular, and not just with cats. Checking them weekly through to early spring, I've found foxes, badgers, owls, a nesting pair of ravens, squirrels, mice, rabbits, and Randy. Twice.

Twenty minutes into the search, the radio crackles. "Think I've got one on the edge of town," Jake mutters.

I get on the radio at once. "Okay, I'm rolling. How far from the road?"

"Not even a block. It's on the plot where they had the gas station fire. Think she's sheltering in an old oil drum."

My face falls as I lock up and start the engine. "Those things have no insulation and are full of toxic crap. I'm on my way."

I focus on the drive down the hill toward town, which

becomes visible once I go around a slight bend. I can see the lot in question: still slightly charred, every bit of bare ground thick with dead weeds. I park near Jake's motorcycle and look around.

Jake is sitting back on his heels on one corner of the shattered blacktop, near a scorched stack of oil drums. His hair licks at his shoulders like a black flame in the wind, and I have to pause and just stare at him. *Beautiful man,* I think as I allow myself to look my fill for once on the way over.

"What have you got?" I ask when I'm about two thirds of the way across the lot. He looks back over his shoulder and puts a gloved finger to his lips in response. I close my mouth and slow down, looking cautiously past him.

A fluffy gray tail drifts back and forth near his boot. I peek around his other side, and see a thin, young, long-haired cat with a loose belly rubbing herself against his hand. *Well I'll be damned.*

"I got close and she just came right over." Indeed she had, and now she was purring audibly and clinging to his ankle. "Someone must have dumped her here."

"Poor baby." I crouch down with him, and the cat shies away for a few moments before coming over to sniff my outstretched hand. Her friendliness is both lucky and heartbreaking; she trusted humans, and look what humans did.

"Do you think we can get her to come with us?" he asks softly, and I nod.

"I don't know how she'll handle us trying to do anything to her babies, but we can try." The corners of my jaw hurt as I let the kitty walk around me, sniffing me. She is purring like a motor—in fact, she seems almost frantic to get our attention.

"Is this normal for strays you pick up?" he asks, his low voice full of fascination. She's practically climbing up his pant leg in her quest for warmth and a good petting.

"Sometimes. Her owner probably dumped her when she

turned up pregnant, and she's done the best she could out here ever since." There's a lump in my throat that won't go away as I turn back toward the truck.

The cat panics as I straighten, and runs up to me, meowing loudly. "It's okay, mama, I'm not going far." But she won't have it. She snags a claw in my pant leg and then jumps down and runs toward the barrels. "Now what?" I mutter, and Jake joins me in following her.

"Oh yeah, she's definitely on board with being rescued," Jake drawls as the cat leaps up into one of the barrels, which holds a thin little nest of rags and newspapers. The desperate mewing inside tells me that she's at least managed to keep her babies alive through the first freezes.

His shoulders block my view into the barrel, and I have to resist a sudden urge to jump onto his broad back for a closer look. "Hey, big guy, I can't see through you."

"I'll count 'em. Hand me your flashlight." He reaches back, and I press it into his huge, gloved hand.

I wait, trying to ignore how his ass looks up close in his tight jeans and failing in the worst way. He's half bent into the barrel with the queen cat meowing at him nervously, but she doesn't hiss, and I stare at the way the denim molds to his muscular cheeks and bulging, rock-hard thighs. *Shit. I need to focus on what I'm doing here.*

"Two, three, four...five. Five kitties. Little bit skinny and shivery, but they're all still alive. You got a carrier big enough for all of them?"

I smile. "Yeah, I brought the big ones along with the other stuff. Do you think we can get the mama cat to cooperate?"

He half straightens and looks over his shoulder at me, eyes dancing. "Are you kidding me?" he replies with a smirk as mama cat hops out of the barrel with a kitten by the scruff and starts carrying her over to my truck.

It's a lucky find: a healthy, docile first litter, even if a little chilled and hungry. None of them particularly like the kennel I bring, as it smells faintly of dog. But once they feel the warm air from the heating pad I slipped in there, Mama starts hauling her kittens into their temporary new digs by the scruff.

We watch until everyone's settled, and I sigh, noticing dried blood on some of the bedding. It's a wonder that she didn't draw predators. Maybe the rust and chemical stink of the drums masked the birthing scent.

Whatever the case, I barely have time for the chill to start sinking through my gloves before we're strapping the crate into my passenger seat. Mama Cat apparently knows what a car ride is, because she's already yowling in irritation. The kittens start mewing, and I giggle a little as I make sure they're secure.

"So where do you need me?" Jake drawls from behind me. I feel his eyes on me and blink. *He's not checking me out, is he?* But no, of course not. *That's a silly idea.*

I should tell him to get back to searching. The weather's going to drop below freezing again tonight, and the threatening rain could turn to snow in a day or two. We can't really spare any time.

"Well, I need to get the babies here settled in one of the isolation rooms and get them and Mama fed and watered. After that I'll be ready to go out and gather more. But..." I hesitate. I don't really *need* his help handling this litter. But...

"If you feel like helping me settle them in, you're welcome. I'll grab some thermoses of coffee for the boys while we're at it." Warmth creeps up my cheeks even as I say it. I'm being selfish and silly, but...I want him with me.

He answers almost too quickly. "Sounds good. And a few thermoses of rocket juice sound good too."

I fight back the urge to beam at him like an idiot. "Yeah. Hopefully all the relocations go this smoothly."

4

CHAPTER FOUR

Jake

"Get it off me!" Tony yells, spinning in an awkward circle while a furious cat clings to the back of his jacket and swats at his ear with one paw. He looks a little bloodied. If it wasn't for the look of sheer panic on his face, I would burst out laughing right there.

The culprit is a tiny but furious mama cat, pure white, with her teeth sunk into Tony's collar. The burly, bearded redhead twirls in place, trying in vain to grab her to pull her off and getting his hands scratched for his trouble.

"All right, all right," I grump, pulling on the heavy gauntlets Kitty retrieved from her truck and walking over to him. "Hold still already!"

"You try holding still while an angry cat's trying to tear your earlobe off!" he yelps, two hundred pounds of biker defeated by six pounds of fuzzy fury.

I do my best to ignore my doubled-over Dad, who is laughing silently with tears streaming down his face. Poor Tony is humiliated enough, and if I pay too much attention I'll start laughing too.

The other guys are looking at the sky, all except for Kitty, who has just wrangled the last of the kittens into the carrier. They're tiny too, and mewing for their mama, but at least now they're out of that deadfall and safe on top of one of the heating pads. "How can anything this little be this fierce?"

"She's one of the smaller breeds, maybe a Singapura mix. The babies are well developed, but they're bitty like her. We have to get all of them inside." She looks up at poor, battered Tony and winces. "Do you guys need a hand?"

"Nah, it's fine, I've got her." I move up behind Tony, who has finally managed to keep still, and grasp the kitty around her midsection—at which point she turns her head and hisses a warning at me as she digs her claws into both of his ears.

"Auuuugh!" he grunts between gritted teeth, and I gingerly pluck them out of his flesh.

"Come on, kitty—" I start, and then she suddenly turns on me in a blur of claws. "Holy fuck!"

I manage to keep hold of her midsection as she twists in my grip and starts lashing all four sets of claws in a blur of desperation and attitude. "Hey! Knock it off, dammit!" I yell, holding her at arm's length as she starts furiously chewing on one of the gauntlets.

"This one's either completely feral or traumatized," Kitty frets, preparing to open the door to the kennel as I walk the little spitfire toward her. I can actually feel the pressure of her little teeth through the thick leather, though she can't break through and get at my skin.

"Yeah, you've got that right. I think she's convinced we want to eat her and her kids." I crouch down beside Kitty and quickly thrust the little hellcat inside. She calms down immediately, refusing to stay violent in close quarters with her kittens. I barely manage to pull the gauntlets out before she bolts for the door. Kitty manages to close it before she can get back out.

"She's really panicked, and she doesn't quite seem to know what to do. I think she's very young." Kitty sounds even more worried now.

I grunt in satisfaction and straighten. "Think Tony's gonna need the liquid bandage for his ear."

I watch a little jealously as Kitty gets Tony to sit down, then cleans the blood off his ear and sprays on the liquid bandage. He winces slightly, but the bleeding stops at once.

I take a peek inside the kennel, and the little hellcat hisses at me—but she's laying down now, her handful of tiny kittens snuggled against her, nursing. "We made sure that's all of them?"

"It's a small litter. Not sure if any of them were stillborn—it's been at least five weeks since the birth. But at least we can save these ones." She shoots me an apologetic look as she packs up her medical gear. "No, looks like they haven't even been here very long. She must have moved them."

It's getting dark. With a hell of a lot of work, we've rescued six litters. Five queens and their litters, plus four orphans we managed to get the other mamas to accept. Forty cats in all. I'm exhausted, the boys are talking Miller Time, and everyone's craving pizza and a smoke.

"We'd better call it for the night," Kitty agrees, though I see the guilt and apprehension on her face. She's so sweet. She's a vet, but even so, she doesn't seem to have fully grasped yet that she can't save them all. "I'll put these guys in an isolation room and get them food and water. Then I need a break."

I eye her. "And then you'll be giving every last one of them a check up between now and when we go back out again tomorrow afternoon?" I let my disapproval creep into my voice, and she blushes and lowers her eyes.

"I have to at least do the basics before I can make room for more animals tomorrow," she ventures, and I shake my head.

"Not alone, you don't. And first let's get you warmed, caffeinated, and filled with some dinner." I give her a pointed look, and she blushes deeper and nods.

"Okay."

"You won't be hearing me say you have an easy job anymore," I admit later. My belly's full of meat-topped pizza and Dad's hard cider, and I'm walking into the shelter with Kitty, determined to make sure she doesn't work too hard.

The complex is separated into two sections: the converted stables in front, where the veterinary clinic is; and the converted barn, now the shelter. The latter is sectioned off into a series of nurseries and isolation rooms, with a grooming center in the back corner. Cats that have already been properly socialized lounge all over the main play area, running up to us and meowing for attention. I give a few a good petting as we make our way toward the first of the isolation rooms.

"Hey Tank, hey Mikey." I scratch the pair of former tomcats on the belly as I go by. I love socializing the fur balls, especially when they're pretty friendly to begin with. I'm not a Cat Whisperer like Kitty, so I'm not so great with the nasty ones.

Kitty looks in through the transparent door at the first group we saved and I come up behind her. Gray Mama has devoured all her food and is sleepily nursing in her heated bed. The litter box has been used, showing this cat's comfort with domestication. She looks up and meows at us, tail drifting calmly.

"I don't think we'll have any problem finding homes for this mama cat and her babies. They will barely need any socialization at all. Just the health stuff." She moves on to the next isolation room almost at once, using a triage process. Some of the other litters are in a lot worse shape, and they need to be helped first.

"Oh yeah, she's a sweetheart. Damn shame that some asshole put her out." The next isolation room has Hellcat in it. She hisses angrily at us and lunges at the door as Kitty crouches down. "Watch out for that one, though."

"She's got one hell of a Napoleon complex. You see it in small dogs too—they get scared by everyone being so huge so they show a lot of attitude." She points at the big, heated shelter-bed where her tiny litter of three is curled up. "But now that she's calming down she's more consistent in taking care of her babies. See how their bellies are all round now?"

"Yeah, guess she could give more milk with clean water and a meal in her belly." Hellcat hisses at us again, but there's less enthusiasm to it. "This one's gonna take a lot of patience and love, Kitty."

"That's okay, I have plenty of both to spare." She smiles at the feisty cat, who finally relaxes enough to peer at her before heading over to her empty food trays. She paws at one, and lets out a tentative meow.

"I noticed," I say, fighting the urge to play with her sleek braid. I can't keep the tenderness out of my tone, and after a moment's pause, she turns back to look at me.

She looks up into my eyes, and for a long, breathless moment I can't tell whether she wants me to kiss her. I stare at her, and finally manage, "Can I ask you a personal question?"

"Um," she murmurs, leaning against the door to face me fully. "Sure, what is it?" Her cheeks are so pink. It's ridiculously adorable.

"How come you don't have guys breaking down your door to go out with you? I've actually wondered that for years." I can't stop smiling now. I may be making the world's stupidest mistake, but I'm happy about it.

She's silent for an alarmingly long time. Then she murmurs, "Oh," as if surprised by my question. "I, um...well...they just don't." Her smile trembles, and I see pain in the backs of her eyes and want to snuff it out at once.

I scratch my neck awkwardly as I straighten up. "I hit a nerve. I'm sorry."

"It's okay. It's just that I'm shy, busy all the time, and, um...not conventional looking." She swallows and goes quiet again, and I feel a surge of anger and grief on her behalf as I think about the ugly treatment that must have caused her shyness. But at least she's not outright saying she's "not conventionally attractive."

"No, you're not conventional looking, but I like that. I think you've run into a lot of idiots over the years who think women should only look one way." *As in, bony underwear models with artificially big boobs.* I'm amazed by how many guys get fantasy and reality so mixed up. But their stupidity is my gain in this case...if I'm very lucky.

"Yeah," she replies in a small voice, but now the note of despair is gone, and she's looking up at me with her big, beautiful eyes.

"Well, for the record, you're fucking beautiful, all right? No bullshit." I don't want to hide my feelings any more, even if I'm overstepping things. Hell, I don't think I can.

"Thank you," she murmurs, and her expression's a little bit baffled. I can't help but crack a grin.

"It's not charity. It's the truth. I just never said a damn thing because...I didn't want to scare you off." We're standing so damn close. I want to pull her into my arms.

She looks up at me, and then moves forward slightly, heat in her eyes. "You don't have to worry about that," she says in that soft, warm voice.

"Your buddy Annabeth doesn't like me too much," I murmur, wondering how much influence her neighbor actually has on Kitty's opinions. It doesn't seem to be much, but...

"Annabeth's scared of who she thinks you are. She's built up some mythology about you and the guys in her head, and it's filled with stereotypes. But I'm not her. I actually know you." She reaches out; just the tiniest gesture, her eyes shy, her fingertips brushing down the open zip of my jacket. "You're the first guy I thought to go to for help. That should...probably tell you something."

That gets me right in the heart, and I move up against her, taking her in my arms. "It does," I murmur.

5

CHAPTER FIVE

Kitty

Jake lifts me off my feet a little as he kisses me. As nice as I find that, it's absolutely necessary. He dwarfs me, and when he hugs me tight against him I'm actually glad of my extra padding. I'm still in shock that he's attracted to me. All this time I thought he only cared about me like I was part of his weird extended family. But then his mouth comes down on mine, and I can't think of anything at all outside of the feeling of his lips on mine.

He's so warm. His hard, rippling chest presses against my breasts, and his fingertips slide over my shoulders and down my back, leaving trails of heat on my skin. His mouth is hot and tastes of cider and spices, and he lets out a little, contented rumble that curls my toes as I kiss him back.

And then the ringer attached to my front doorbell goes off. I freeze.

He breaks the kiss, grumbling. "You have to be kidding me."

I sigh, blushing down to my toes as if I'm fourteen and my mom just caught me smooching the neighborhood bad boy. But then again, it's been a while since I've had a proper kiss—and no kiss I've ever received has been as proper as the one I just got.

I'd rather go back in for seconds, but whoever's out front is leaning on the doorbell now like it's some kind of emergency. We both look over at the flashing signal light that accompanies it, and I shake my head. "I had better go see who it is."

"Dammit," he grumbles—good-naturedly, given the circumstances. I can completely sympathize.

"Yeah," I grumble back as I head back out the door toward the house. The doorbell keeps buzzing and buzzing and I bite back the urge to yell at whoever it is. "Of all the goddamn times for some jackass to interrupt me," I growl under my breath as I stomp around the corner of the house.

Annabeth is standing there, awkwardly holding her coat closed over her housecoat, her hair in curlers and her eyes full of fear. My anger fades away immediately as I catch the panic in her face, and I hurry over. "Hey, what is it? Is everything all right?"

"That's what I was going to ask you!" she gasps out, looking me over. "Those bikers have been coming around your property, and I saw one of their motorcycles parked in your driveway and just thought…"

My heart sinks. *Goddamn it.* "Annabeth, honey, it isn't like that at all. You know how I asked you if I could search your land for kittens tomorrow?"

She calms slightly. "Um…no? Wait. Yes. Yes, you did bring it up, that was a little after lunchtime." Then she blinks at me in confusion. "But what does that have to do with those…criminals? Did they do anything to you? Are you in trouble? Do you need to come over to my place to hide?"

"Oh, Annabeth." I want to hug her tight and beat her with a pool noodle at the same time. *Idiot. Lovable idiot.* "No, honey, no. Just…look. I needed help. A lot of help, fast. Jake and his men owe me because I take care of their dogs, and so I asked them."

Annabeth blinks at me slowly, and for a moment I think that it's all going to sink in. "They were helping you rescue...kittens?"

"Five mama cats and forty-five kittens. You can come by tomorrow morning and see them for yourself once I've had a chance to give them all check-ups. If you have room in your home for a coyote, well...you keep telling me Mittens wants someone to play with."

Her eyes light up and I feel another little tentative bit of hope. "Well, I would like to see the kitties. But not while those...bikers...are around. I really don't know about using them as volunteers, sweetie. I never liked that you go over there so much. They're dangerous people."

"Annabeth, look, I know that your heart is in the right place," I start beseechingly, because I'm tired of this and want to go back to Jake's arms. It was a good day, even if we didn't rescue all the cats out there. That kiss...made it so much better, and in its wake, Annabeth's disapproval stings.

"But what?" she snaps. Her eyes seem fixed on my mouth suddenly. "If you're about to patronize me, don't."

"I think you know me a little better than that," I sigh, and her defensive look softens.

"Well, what is it, then?" She's staring at my mouth. I'm certain of it, and her scrutiny makes me squirm inside.

I calm myself by counting to ten before answering. "Have you ever even had a conversation with any of them? Jake's father Spike is a vet, and very—"

"Of course I haven't spoken to any of them," Annabeth cuts in quickly. "They're too dangerous for a woman to be around on her own; that's the whole reason I'm so worried about you right now."

I rub my face, too aware of the chill and the way my lips still tingle, sensitized by the touch of Jake's mouth. "Look, even if you don't trust them, you can trust me. Have I ever steered you wrong?"

She puts her chubby little hands on her hips, and I suddenly realize that I'm in for more of a lecture than I expected. "Well, you know, normally I would trust you. But this time it's pretty clear your judgment is off, sweetie."

My heart starts beating faster, part from worry about what she's going to do and part from fighting the urge to just smack her silly. All those pointless, unprovoked phone calls to police...and now she's acting like something's wrong with me too. "What do you mean?"

"Your lipstick's smeared, and you've been alone in the barn with that...that gang leader! What is this? Are you completely crazy? The man is a criminal!" She even flaps her arms a little for emphasis.

That's when I reach my limit. I'm not normally an aggressive person, especially with Annabeth, but the tide of anger that rises up inside of me feels like a volcano about to blow. "Annabeth, stop making stuff up and believing it's true! The man's got nothing on his record more serious than blowing through a stop sign, and you can check that for yourself!"

She huffs at me angrily, her eyes flashing. "You just think this 'Big Jake' is cute so you want to cover for him!"

"I don't have to cover for him! I have a barn full of rescue kittens that says he's not what you think he is." I actually raise my voice a little. "And the Ravens go out of their way not to disturb you even though you've used the police to harass them for years! In fact, if Jake's dad didn't think that *you're* cute, Jake probably would have told you where to shove it by now!"

She pauses, blinking, and her hands slip off her hips in her surprise. "Spike Steele thinks I'm cu—oh, never mind that! I'm worried about you, Kitty! Those men may be nice to you now, but they're only waiting for you to let your guard down."

"They've been waiting for years? To do what? Annabeth, please. I'm cold, and I have a lot of work to do on those cats. Can't you just—" I break off. *I'm so tired of this.*

"Oh, don't talk to me about your responsibilities, you ridiculous girl. You know that's not why you're so eager to get back to what you were doing. As soon as you disappear back into the barn with that gang's...leader, he'll be kissing off the rest of your makeup, I just know it!"

I freeze, staring at her. *Uh oh.* For once, her crazy theory is actually half right, which will probably make her feel even more justified. "Okay, that's it. I'm going to have to ask you to get off my property and go home."

Her jaw drops. She seems oblivious to just how far out of line she's being, so blinded by her good intentions that she's not looking at the effects her actions have on others. We stare at each other, with me fighting the regret welling up inside of me.

Finally, she turns on her heel and hobbles away, not looking back once as she heads up toward the road.

I watch her until she disappears into the gloom, and shake my head, my heart in my shoes. I feel like I've just lost Annabeth as a friend, but that isn't the worst of it. I know this isn't the end of this, and I'm suddenly very, very worried about what she might be planning.

CHAPTER SIX

Jake

After that kiss, even the bullshit with Annabeth can't kill my mood—or ruin what's blooming between me and sweet Kitty.

We've brought in every litter we could find over the last couple weeks. Now we're dealing with the long process of checking, grooming, immunizing, feeding, and socializing a grand total of seventy-eight kittens, nine mama cats and one injured tom. But I don't mind one bit of the extra work, as long as I can spend time with her.

I have to take it slow with this little lady, which is excruciating but delicious all at once. It's not enough that she has a crush on me and wants to have sex because she thinks it's what I expect. I want her to want it so much that I can coax her past some of her shyness.

We steal kisses while we work in the shelter, while the boys, Dad, and I help her get her Christmas lights up, and every night before we both bed down. Every time, we go a little further, like horny teens testing the waters with each other, bit by sneaky bit.

We hide it from the Ravens, we hide it from the other volunteers that come in from town to feed and tend to the kittens, and we're even careful in private, because Annabeth has gotten even nosier.

It's hard to ignore someone who camps out across the road from your house and watches your comings and goings with a pair of binoculars and a video recorder—especially when she keeps sneaking onto our land and setting the dogs off barking. It would actually be funny and cute if it wasn't awkward as hell, leaving Kitty and I feeling even more like we have to sneak around.

In a way though, the sneaking around makes things even more amazing. It's forced us to draw things out, making us limit the things we can do with one another, as if we're teenagers sneaking around behind our parents' backs. I get hard as a rock just thinking about kissing Kitty. Sex with her will definitely be worth the wait.

Meanwhile, I've got a wannabe spy in pink chenille and purple Wellies sneaking around my bushes.

"She's back again." Dad's eyes are dancing. He's the only one of us who is happy about this development. In fact, his mood has picked up a lot since she started coming around and giving him an excuse to "confront" her.

Outside, by one of the windows, I hear a rustle and a yelp as our visitor trips into a hedge. I grumble and set down my beer. "I'm getting the hose."

Three of the guys start snickering, and Dad laughs and levers himself out of his chair. "No, no, don't you go doing something we'll feel guilty about in the morning. I'll go talk to her."

"If it's a date she wants, why can't she just get your damn phone number and stay out of our bushes?" I'm still grumbling, but it's more good-natured. Across from me, Lars, a new pledge with an agricultural science degree, is turning red and choking into his hand, blond hair flopping across his face.

"I'll see if I can convince her!" My Dad pulls his fleece-lined jacket on and zips it before going outside. He's humming and tugging on his gloves as he closes the door.

I shake my head and stop fighting my grin. This crap is annoying, and we're going to have to find a way around it. But...right now, Dad's happy—something that hasn't happened often enough lately. He's also providing Annabeth with the perfect distraction as I grab my own jacket and slip out the back.

It's a week before Christmas now, and the weather's gone from crisp to ball-shrinkingly cold at night. A thin crust of snow covers everything, reflecting the moonlight with a pale, bluish glow.

Everyone's got their lights up, as much for road safety in this dark stretch of mountain road as its ability to pierce the gloom and because it looks pretty. Even our big front hedges are covered in twinkling, multicolored lights, which look like thousands of psychedelic fireflies. Since we started doing that two years ago, the drunken holiday drivers who take a wrong turn through our hedge have gone from a few a year to none.

The lights are still on over at the shelter, meaning that my sweet little lady is still hard at work. *Big surprise there.* I head to the shelter door, wondering where the heck Kitty gets her energy from. She claims she takes a lot of naps scattered throughout the day, and it leaves me wondering if I should try that myself. But I still catch her yawning as I walk inside.

She's crouching at the open door of one of the isolation rooms, holding her fingers out for Hellcat. That angry little kitty, along with her babies, is discovering the joys of being warm, clean, free of fleas, and well fed. Kitty yawns into her fist, eyes squinting closed—and the white ball of razors, fluff, and attitude spies me and comes bounding over.

I don't know how it is that over the last few weeks, Hellcat decided I was hers. Maybe it was because of all the time I spent here, or because I let her kids climb on me, or maybe because I don't put up with her shit. But I crouch down, and with a few scrambles and leaps, she's perched on my shoulder, kneading the leather and purring up a storm.

"Hey, Hellcat." I give her a good scratching. Now that the fleas and filth are gone and she's had weeks of good meals, she's gone from ratty as old couch stuffing to a fluffy white fairy-kitty —who could still destroy a person if she wanted to. I look up at Kitty and give her a smile. "Hey, Angel Cat."

"Hey Jake." She always looks a little flushed and bright-eyed when I'm around her these days, like she can't quite believe the direction things have gone between us. She's so overwhelmed by everything—every kiss, every touch—that I've slowly come to realize that before me, she was totally untouched.

Yet another reason for me to take it easy and slow, and to savor every moment with her. First times only come around once, and I really want to take care of her. So even though her kiss hello has me wanting to press her back against a wall and leave her riding my thigh, I just tease her braid a little before letting her go.

"So what's the latest?" I stifle a yawn. *The damn things really are contagious.*

"Well, I have homes for thirty-nine of the kittens and two of the mama cats. We're breaking up the families as little as possible, but they all have to get the rest of their immunizations and get sterilized before we send them out. I'm hoping to get the first round of kittens to their new homes by the twenty-third. That's nine going home." She steals another kiss and her wonderfully soft, curvy body brushes against mine as she moves past me to collect Hellcat's kittens.

"These guys have gained an average of seven ounces, which

is a little behind the curve." She reaches over to pet Hellcat, who purrs and leans into her hand. Her three babies came to us the size of hamsters, and we're doing our best to help them gain weight. So far, so good.

"Any of them turn up with any real health problems?" The yearling tomcat, a skinny black thing who had stuck by his mother, had a badly-healed back leg that Kitty had been forced to correct with surgery. He is hobbling around on a cast now, and is already a pound heavier.

His is the worst problem I know about, but you never really know for sure until you have the test results back. Labs are notoriously bad at sending reports back on time in rural areas, especially during the holidays—or so Kitty tells me.

"Well, besides the fleas and a late-season tick or two, and the one litter passing around some low-grade sniffles, we're okay. Some of them have scars, some needed their claws trimmed, and some still need their teeth cleaned, including Hellcat." She rolls her eyes as Hellcat's kittens climb onto her shoulders, claws digging into her green and red ugly Christmas sweater.

I laugh. "That's gonna be an adventure. How do you plan to manage it?"

"Maybe I'll get the kittens used to it too, so she'll see them go through it and come out all right. She may attack my legs again while I'm doing their teeth, but I'll wear my over-the-knee boots."

"You should wear those anyway, they're sexy," I say in a teasing voice, and she laughs and ducks her head. I catch her chin with two fingers, very gently, and coax her head up. "I'm not kidding," I purr at her, and watch her eyes dilate as her knees get just a bit wobbly.

She's like a love-struck teen. It's adorable. I am smiling down at her and ready to lean in for another kiss when suddenly the lights go out.

The darkness that drops down over my vision is so profound that for a second I think I've gone blind—but then I realize what has happened. The distant heavy clunk that accompanies our plunge into total darkness tells me that this is more than a blown fuse. So do the faint curses I hear outside and down the hill at our place.

"Shit," Kitty growls as we both pull flashlights off our belts. A moment later, the emergency lights kick on, sending a faint amber glow over everything.

"Blackout. Great." It's another part of winter that has come far too early—the regular, usually short failures of our power grid. I put a hand on her shoulder to help her steady herself. "What heating system is this building on?"

"Natural gas hydronics, both in-floor and through radiators. The gas isn't interrupted, so we'll have heat as long as we can run the thermostat. The problem is electricity—lights, thermostat, computers, phone charging, and most of my lab equipment run on building power." She takes several steadying breaths.

"What about your generators?"

"The ones for the shelter are new, though I have to check their fuel levels. But the generators for the main house are both off-line. I didn't have time to get them fixed before this early winter bullshit happened. Not on top of everything else." She can't keep the frustration out of her voice.

"Okay, look. You keep getting the cats sorted out as best you can. I'll go kick on the generators for in here and check your fuel levels, then go over to the main house and start bringing us back some food and bedding. We can sleep in here tonight, keep the cats company."

She blinks at me several times, then says haltingly, "That...that sounds good, Jake."

I don't understand why she's staring at me wide-eyed until we bundle Hellcat and her boys into their room and I am on my way out the door. As I step out into the cold night again, it suddenly hits me. I just told her that I'm staying the night with her.

And she just agreed.

Holy shit.

I walk around toward the generator shed with a big smile on my face, not feeling the cold at all.

CHAPTER SEVEN

Kitty

It shouldn't come as a surprise to me at this point, but Jake sure knows how to take charge. Three minutes after he walks out I hear the rumble of the generators starting up, and suddenly the lights flicker back on. I smile, heart still pounding a little over what I just agreed to so easily. *He's staying the night.*

And apparently, he wants to stay the night in relative comfort.

I'm shocked when Jake's idea of "bringing some bedding back" starts with an entire guest room mattress coming through the shelter door, with Jake grunting and shoving at the far end. I run forward to help, and we pull it through onto the heated concrete floor between the isolation rooms.

The free-range cats are meowing at us and milling around the room, unused to the lights going out so early. They are just as confused as I am. But when Jake sighs and straightens, turning to face me, I see his exasperated expression and know he has some news. "What is it?" I ask him as he frowns and glances back at the door.

"Well, I've got some bad news. The temperature's dropping fast as hell, and as it turns out, we had a transformer go out between here and town. That means it will be at least until morning before anyone can get out here. Maybe another half day after that to get the new transformer in, fix any problems the failure caused, and move on.

"Now, I can run you some fuel from our stockpile if you need some for the generators, but we'll still have to stretch it. Make sure that it gets used for heating, cooking, vet equipment, stuff like that." He snorts, seeing the half a dozen cats that have already hopped onto the mattress and flopped down.

"You make it sound like it might be days." I couldn't keep the worry out of my voice. The heat was functioning, but the thermostat was not, and neither were the heater's electronic components. Not without power.

"Well, they don't like the bad publicity of making local people go without power on the holidays, but that doesn't mean they won't let a small number of us slide because they're shorthanded for the same damn reason." He looks at me, his face full of concern. "You're worried about running out of generator fuel and not being able to fire the heater."

My heart sinks. Growing up, I was so sickly that I stayed home a ton, and my cats were often my only real company. I got…attached. Now, thinking of all these kittens we've rescued who are now at risk of freezing all over again, I start to shake.

"Oh shit. Hey, hey, hey, don't do that. Don't freak out." Jake steps forward and pulls me against his massive chest, the scent of leather, sweat, and a hint of pot mixing in my nostrils as I cling to him. "It'll be okay."

I let out a small sob of frustration and anxiety and bury my face against him. The early winter, Annabeth, getting all the cats ready for adoption, trying to find them homes...it has all taken its toll. Now the blackout has added to that, and even though Jake is here with me, I'm at the end of my rope.

But as he holds me, his heat starts sinking into me and my body relaxes a little. His arms settle around me and he strokes his hand over the back of my head until I relax even more, and the tears stop pushing at the backs of my eyes. "There you go," he murmurs—as a set of sharp claws starts making their way up my leg, over my hip and up my side.

I blink and look down into a pair of wide blue-green eyes. The Siamese kitten lets out a giant meow, and Jake starts laughing silently, shaking against me. "It'll be fine," he purrs in my ear as he plucks the kitten from my clothes and sets it on his shoulder. "I promise."

We keep working, using as few lights and electrical equipment as we can. Now and again I hear the heater kicking back on as it fights the chill seeping through the building's brick walls and thick insulation. When I get overwhelmed, which keeps happening because I'm so tired and stressed, he's right there for me. Eventually, I recover enough that I can start looking forward to this whole "staying over" thing again.

I could be reading this wrong. He could just want to keep me safe in the middle of this whole mess. There are some real creeps living close enough that you never know who might try to take advantage of something like this. Now and again one of them decides to slip up into the hills during a storm or blackout to see who might be naïve enough to leave their doors unlocked.

Jake could just be acting chivalrous. Except...

Except as my heart calms and I nestle against him, I can't help but notice the throbbing boulder pushing into my belly. His jeans are doing nothing to hide it, and I can feel him clearly even through my layers of clothing. It's almost alarming how huge he is, and I suddenly realize one *really big* reason why he's been taking it so slow with my tiny, inexperienced ass.

Well...damn. I am suddenly blushing from my collarbones up, and trying not to giggle.

"What is it?" he rumbles curiously. He lets me go because more cats are yelling for food and we move to remedy the situation, filling bowls and topping off the water fountains. As we work, I'm still struggling not to giggle. "C'mon, what?"

Well, sweetie, I just figured out that you're packing the Washington Monument. Give me a second, I'll be fine... "Um. It's nothing, I'm just trying to see the funny side of all this."

"That's probably a good thing," he chuckles as he tears open another bag of cat food. The chorus of meows is so ridiculous that I wish I could spare a bit of power to record it. "Good thing cats don't give a shit if it's dark. I bet the dogs are panicking."

"They'll just need to know where everyone is. Especially Chewie." I can't hear his booming barks from over here, though, so I suspect Spike's taking care of him. Then I hesitate. "I should go check on Annabeth."

"Shit." He grumbles, but then lets out a sigh. "You're right, she's up there alone." He turns a look my way. "I guess you don't want me coming with?"

"She'll freak out. I don't like being out there alone in the dark, but...if I have any more drama tonight I'll just be done." I frown. I don't want to take one second away from Jake and my work to deal with Annabeth. The lady has managed to alienate me a hell of a lot these past couple weeks, no matter how good her intentions.

Duty calls, though. I've always been a good neighbor—even when Annabeth doesn't deserve it with her annoying but well intentioned snooping.

"Okay. But, uh...while you're over there, could you ask her to stay out of my bushes? Dad likes it, but they need to go on a real date instead of...that. You know?" He nuzzles a kiss into the top of my head.

I chuckle a little as I bundle up and grab my big flashlight. One lingering kiss later, and I reluctantly walk out into the cold.

The whole area looks...eerie...with no lights on. Now and again, the slice of winding highway downhill lights up through the pines with brief flashes as a set of headlights races past. There are generators humming away in the gloom up and down the hill, and as I step out into the road to get a better view, I see that Jake's place and Annabeth's both have faint lights in their windows.

I smile with relief. *She must be fine.* But I know I should still check on her, so I start trudging up the hill, carefully hugging the shoulder of the road.

A sharp bark catches my attention and my head snaps around. I see the faint pale shape of a fat coyote standing on the other side of the road, right before the blind curve just beyond Annabeth's house. "Oh hey Randy—" I start before being cut off by the rising rumble of a motor as a dark shape races toward me, blocking the coyote from sight.

Fuck.

I throw myself into the woods just in time—a speeding SUV with its lights off roars past me, just inches from my legs. The hot wind from the machine throws me off balance and sprays bits of dead leaves and road grit into my face. I grab a tree and hang on, panting in shock as the drunk driver goes weaving down the road, brake lights never even flickering.

Oh God, I almost died. If Randy hadn't gotten my attention—but I can't even finish that thought before I start sobbing.

A little while later, I hear heavy, booted footsteps approach. They stop near my flashlight, which lies a few feet away from my shivering, balled-up form. A gloved hand picks it up and flashes it around. I squint as the light falls over me.

I know it's Jake by his scent as he stows the flashlight and scoops me into his arms. I cling to him and just let him carry me back to the shelter, my chest hitching and my cheeks cold from tears.

It takes me a long time to recover, and by the time I do, he has my coat, vest, and boots off, and he's cuddling with me in the nest of comforters and pillows he's piled onto the mattress. He kicks off his boots as he cradles me, sighing into my hair. "You okay?" he asks finally. "Did you fall?"

"No," I mumble as I tuck my head under his chin. "There was a drunk guy driving with his headlights off outside in this mess and he almost hit me." I leave out the bit about Randy, because that part is a little too weird for me and I'm not calm or stoned enough to tell it yet.

"Jesus," he mumbles, horrified. "Any idea what the car looked like?"

"Black SUV, no lights, barely touched his brakes. No idea who it was, but I doubt they're actually from around here." I hope, anyway. If I ever actually caught whoever drove that vehicle, I would probably kick his ass. Jake, despite being gentle with me, radiates protective anger right now, and I know he would be perfectly willing to back me up when it came time for that ass-kicking.

And that could land both of us in jail, so...not a good idea at all.

Maybe, if I ever find the bastard, I'll just sue him silly. I can certainly afford a good lawyer now. And anyone who drives a new SUV with no lights down a mountain road has to be rich enough that replacing it wouldn't be a burden, so I don't feel at all bad about the idea.

"I'll have my guys go looking for that goddamn idiot in town tomorrow," he growls, and I feel a strange mix of flattery, shock, worry, and horniness.

"Jake...wait. If we do anything about this guy, I want to find out his name and address so I can serve him with a lawsuit." It's such a city-girl thing to say that I'm a little shocked as the words come out of my mouth.

He blinks down at me...then nods. "I can understand that. But if you want to sue you'll have to file a police report. It'll be asked about, especially since you almost got seriously hurt."

He's petting my hair slowly, meditatively...and then he's slipping the band off my braid and gently undoing it. A tingle shoots down from my scalp and all the way to my toes. I let out a low gasp.

"I'll...deal with that in the morning," I mumble. The tingling settles in my nipples and I feel them tighten into points, growing maddeningly sensitive in seconds. My knees clench together, and the tight press of denim against my crotch makes things even worse.

I don't know how Jake manages it, but the safety I feel in the circle of his arms is the perfect antidote to my crazy brush with death, and all the adrenaline it's shot into my system. That terrible moment when I was almost crushed to death by the SUV is fading into the back of my head like a quickly receding nightmare. I lay my cheek against his chest and hear the soft thunder of his heart in my ear.

It's time says something inside of me, and apprehension mixes with anticipation, tightening my guts and leaving my heart pounding. My cheeks are so flushed that my tears dry quickly, leaving my skin tight in their absence.

We kiss for a long time while he runs his hands through my loosened hair, and my fingertips explore his chest and shoulders through his shirt. The territory is growing more familiar, but exploring the planes and curves of his muscled body never gets old.

Part of me keeps threatening to seize up from self-consciousness, even though he always tells me that I'm beautiful, and I know he'll never hurt me. Logic doesn't help against this feeling, not really. I can only power through it—and the soft, almost lazy kisses and caresses he lays on me as I curl up in his lap give me the fuel to do just that.

He breathes hard as his lips run over my jawline. Impatient, I strip off my sweater and toss it aside. His hands start to caress me through the thin silk of my turtleneck, leaving behind a trail of goosebumps on my skin that only hunger for more contact.

My body has been starved for contact for years, even when I wasn't alone. Years of slobbery kisses, boob grabs when I least expected them, and dates that ended quickly on discovering that the guy in question was just hoping the big girl would be desperate enough to be easy. Years of not going through with sex just because the right guy wasn't around.

Now, here he is. *Am I ready for this?*

I had better be. The roller coaster is ticking up the first slope, and the ride is about to begin.

We're both starting to get impatient now, breaths shivering and hands fumbling to help each other undress. He peels off his shirt and undershirt, throwing them aside, and I lean forward to kiss and nuzzle his chest as I run my palms up and down his rippled, lightly furred belly.

He hisses through his teeth with pleasure, his thick fingers sliding through my hair and up and down my back. I can feel his heartbeat pick up as I raise my arms and let him pull the turtleneck off over my head.

The warm press of his skin on mine as he takes me in his arms and we lie down sideways on the makeshift bed makes me stretch up against him, pressing closer, wanting to feel more of him. His hands move down past the small of my back, cupping my ass and sliding up and down over and over as we kiss and tangle up together.

We end up rolling around on the bedding, my heart pounding harder and harder as his hands slide over my bare skin, as he works to bare more. I unbuckle my pants for him and lift my hips so he can pull them off, not caring that I'm in my underwear now. I feel brazen; when his huge body covers mine there's no room for self-consciousness.

I can hear his breathing, harsh in my ear as he loosens his belt and unzips his fly halfway to give that giant in his pants some room. I have to squash a surge of apprehension as I catch sight of it again. Growing daring, I reach to unzip his fly as we lay our heads on a pillow—only to encounter a round lump that hisses and bolts.

We both freeze for a moment before Jake chuckles. "Shit," he mutters in my ear, and I giggle in spite of myself. Then he kisses me again, managing to be rough and tender all at once, his hot mouth distracting me from the cat-related awkwardness.

I have never felt like this before. My whole body is feverish with need, and the self-consciousness that was dragging me down before has now dissolved completely. When he undoes the catch on my bra, I don't bother reaching up to hide my nipples in my palms. I just let the straps slide down off my arms, and look up at him as he gazes in awe at my ample breasts.

"God, baby," he purrs. "Those are definitely worth the wait."

I let out a little cry of startled pleasure as he lunges forward to bury his face between them, and I cradle his head against my body. His kisses and the soft scratch of his stubble feel so good...and then he closes his mouth over my nipple and everything seems to blur around me.

I let out a low wail and cling to him, rocking back and forth as he suckles me. The pleasure is so intense that it almost hurts. The pleasure is electric, running outward from my nipple in jolts. The intensity makes me shiver violently, and I moan and whisper, in a tiny pleading voice, that he can't stop.

An ache has started between my thighs; my cunt throbs and grows moist with a hunger I've only ever felt in passing before. One of his hands kneads my other breast as he crouches over me, his huge palm engulfing most of my breast. The warmth from his mouth and his palm sink into me, and I arch up against him and bury my hands in his hair.

He lets out an almost agonized grunt and switches to my other breast; his bulging groin sliding against my leg as he latches on. My hands slide down from his hair and dig into his shoulders as my mind goes hazy and I start to moan aloud.

He slides my panties off as he works me over, and starts kneading my ass firmly in time with the movements of his mouth. I grind my hips reflexively as he starts running his mouth down the small mound of my belly, slowly moving lower.

Oh my God, he's going to—

I seize up, trying not to slam my legs closed on reflex, and my eyes widen so much they hurt. When his breath blows warm over the tiny, sparse hairs on my cunt, I can't get enough air in my lungs. My fingers dig into the bedding on either side of me so hard that I know my nails would be gouging his skin if I hung on. He lifts me by the hips...and then his tongue starts working between the lips of my pussy and my eyes roll closed.

The lashing of his tongue makes me jolt in time to his movements; my whole body seizing up and trembling, relaxing only a little between strokes. A tremendous pressure grows in my womb, like a balloon swelling up to the point of bursting. I become an animal, clawing at the bedding, at his shoulders, at the air, as he patiently explores my folds and then settles in for a real feast.

My toes crack as they curl and I go up on my heels; my whining gasps growing into a long, almost painful cry broken up only by my desperate pants. Every stroke of his tongue drives me further and further, until I feel something give and my pleasure detonates through me in waves of fire.

For long heartbeats, I'm suspended; time stops, and my body writhes under the onslaught of a pleasure I've never felt. Spasm after spasm runs through me...and then it all ebbs away again, leaving me blissfully exhausted.

I collapse to the mattress, sobbing for air, my body limp and tingling, as he lifts his head and climbs up over me. I hear a rustle as he sheds his jeans, and this time I'm too stunned by the climax I've never felt before for the apprehension to hit.

My thighs are already parted; my cunt relaxed and receptive. I feel the push of something huge, smooth and throbbing between my pussy lips—and then it starts to slide into me as he gasps tremulously into my ear. I lift my hips, pushing back, and it hurts a little as his girth stretches me and he sinks in deep. But only a little.

"Ohh. Oh, baby, yeah—you feel so fucking good," he groans as he pushes deep, then draws out and sinks into me again. He moves so slowly, drawing out and sinking in, his motions smooth and gentle as my body gets used to his presence. The effort of holding back makes him shake.

Gradually he speeds up, hips working against me, his gasps harsh in my ear as his hips push mine into the mattress over and over. I can hear the springs creak with each thrust; he nearly bottoms out at times from his enthusiasm. But never once past the first few seconds does it hurt.

His tremors and groans, the churning of his hips against me, the push of his cock and the way he presses his weight into me until I sink into the mattress—it all starts stoking up my pleasure again. It doesn't take long before I'm hanging on for dear life and whimpering into his shoulder.

I look up and see his eyes screwed closed, his lips parted and an expression of near awe on his face. Then my body takes over and I grind against him with all my strength, feeling my cunt contract around him even tighter than before. He stiffens—and then thrusts deep, his cock jolting inside of me in time to his harsh, panting shouts.

We float back down to earth together, his weight settling over me comfortingly as I struggle to catch my breath. For long moments, he is silent and limp, and I wonder if I actually managed to knock him out with pleasure. The idea is incredibly flattering—but of course, also silly.

After a while, he drags his head up and loosens his grip on me. My flesh aches a little where his hands rest; I may have finger bruises later. He seems a little ashamed of that, asking at once, "You okay?"

It takes me a few dizzy moments before I can form words. I smile up at him while I do my best. "I'm more than okay. By a lot."

A tired grin flashes across his face as he lays his head on my shoulder. "Good. Me too."

CHAPTER EIGHT

Jake

The road crew from the power company manages to get the power back on at mid-afternoon the next day. Kitty and I look after the cats and each other until then, and spend the rest of our time in bed.

I CAN'T REMEMBER the last time it felt this good to have a woman under me, beside me, lying over me—exhausted, sobbing, and trembling with ecstasy as I thrust my cock deep into her body. She's so soft and warm and responsive, and no matter how tired she is by the time I empty myself into her, she always holds me, rolling her hips to draw the last spasms out of me.

IT FEELS INCREDIBLE, making me yell like a teen who's never gone balls deep before. *God, she's a fast learner* I think as I settle over her for the fourth time that day, lungs burning from the effort of screwing us both silly. It takes actual time and effort to make myself roll off her and pull her against me, instead of drowsing off again right there on top of her.

She's sleeping peacefully when the lights come back on. I squint up into the sudden brightness and sigh, reluctantly sitting up. The generators need to be turned off and everything needs to be checked, and she's been working too hard. I won't disturb her.

My skin actually tingles as I pull on my jeans. I haven't gotten laid this thoroughly in years. It's enough to make even me a little wobbly. And it definitely puts me in a good mood, even as I plod around in the cold without my coffee or wake and bake.

I hope everything's all right down at our place, but I'll have to check after I take care of things up here. The guys will have things covered at the clubhouse. But I do take a look down the road after turning off the generators and restoring main power to the heating system.

My eyebrows rise as I catch sight of activity down the road. *Well, that explains why the power's out.* There's a repair crew working a quarter mile down from the clubhouse, currently hauling a mangled truck and the chunks of the power pole it shattered up the slope with winches. There's a coroner's truck just beyond that is closing up to leave.

The transformer didn't blow; it's lying on its side at the edge of the road with traffic cones in a ring around it. I can only imagine how fast that truck was going when it hit the pole, or how drunk the driver was. It chills my blood to see—I know he or she has to be the one in the body bag I glimpsed.

IT MUST HAVE TAKEN *them the whole morning to pry the body out of that wreck.* Worse, there's a second vehicle upended against a tree just a little down from there: a black SUV. My mind does the math, and I realize that it has to be the person who almost hit my Kitty last night. I can't feel too bad about that.

I'M JUST glad they have the new pole up and the new transformer connected. I do hope they get the wreckage dragged away before Kitty's up and around outside. She doesn't need to see this mess.

ONE THING ANNOYS me as I turn to go back inside: Annabeth's pink dressing gown and purple coat, and the gleam of her camera, are once again planted right on the edge of my property, recording. At least this time she's pointing her camera toward the cleanup. But I'm sure that in her head, we're somehow responsible for both the drunks and the blackout.

SHAKING MY HEAD, I plod back toward the shelter and a pile of work—and my sleeping sweetheart, whom I would pounce on for another round if it wasn't time to deal with the cats. *Duty calls.* But...there will be plenty of time for more sex afterward.

. . .

I'm really looking forward to that.

Two days to Christmas, and everything's as ready as it's going to be for those nine cats to get to their new homes. Kitty has made sure that people know where they were found, telling everyone that the local gang of tough guys actually helped rescue these fur balls.

She says that it's just as important for the locals to know we're good people as it is to know that we're badass, and she's right. It's not like we're defending turf in the big city, and our cash crop's legal and licensed now. *If Annabeth could see us now,* I think proudly as I watch Chewie patiently endure a fluffy black kitten clambering over his face.

People are never just one thing. Kitty herself can be tough as hell when she needs to be, and me...I can be a pretty cushy teddy bear when I'm with the right people. I don't mind any more if it gets out—I'm not twenty, and the people I need to respect me already do. Besides, if we ever have kids, I don't want them to be afraid of me, right?

I pause, blinking over at Kitty as she stuffs the last of the stockings. *I just thought about having kids with her. Whoa. Holy shit.*

It's a question for the future, though, not for now. I know that. And after waiting years to say something and a month to make love to her, I can be patient.

. . .

We're not expecting it, but come three in the afternoon, when our adopters are supposed to arrive, we find ourselves with a line running all the way from the shelter to the back of the parking lot. Lots of kids, lots of families. It almost looks like an entire neighborhood has come down for kitten therapy.

"My family was in town," explains Aaron Chiu, from in town, on his way through the door. "They heard we were surprising my wife with a cat and two of her babies, and they wanted to see the other kittens." He looks a little surprised to see a big biker at the door, and cranes his head around to try and look past me into the shelter. "Is...this the right place?"

Suddenly the tiny, black-haired cherub holding hands with him giggles and points at me. I hear the tiny picking sound of my clothes being used as a ladder, and then a small, purring weight settles on my shoulder. The guy relaxes considerably, and some of the other kids laugh.

"Uh, yeah, I'd say you're in the right place," I say a little sheepishly as Hellcat plants herself on me and head-butts my ear. I step aside. "Come on in."

"Where did they all come from?" Kitty breathes as the main room of the shelter fills up with folks from town—and out of town. We were proactive and shut the cats in the various isolation and interaction rooms so that none of them could sneak out while people were going in and out. But neither of us expected this kind of crowd.

"Looks like everybody's got their family in town for the holidays," I reply in a slightly baffled voice. So far two families have left with their kitties, while everyone else is hanging out drinking hot drinks, chatting and playing with the cats and kittens. It's nice...especially since four of them have already signed up to adopt kitten pairs when they're ready to be rehomed, and two more are interested in adults.

Whatever is going on, I'm grateful for it, and from the look on her face, so is Kitty. But it's quickly getting a little exhausting after everything that has happened. Not to mention all the fucking we've been doing in the last day and a half.

The crowd has finally trickled out, the kittens have gone home, two volunteers have signed up to help at the shelter and there's a small stack of adoption applications sitting on the counter by the time the sun sets. The guys and my dad are hanging out, eagerly waiting for pizza, Kitty's brewing the coffee, and I'm digging two longnecks out of the mini fridge when we hear a hard, authoritative knock on the door.

I can't help but stiffen, as do some of the guys. That's a knock from a cop; anyone who has ever had friends on the wrong side of the law knows it well. Kitty looks up in alarm, and I move to get the door, but she shakes her head. "I'll get it," she says firmly.

It's probably a good idea. I look like trouble to the average cop, even though the locals know that Annabeth is full of shit. Kitty practically has "cuddle me" tattooed on her forehead. People tend to trust her at once.

She hurries over to the door and opens it—and two hulking uniformed cops look in past her with awkward but curious expressions. No hostility. Maybe a little confusion. That's an expression I've gotten used to from these guys, and I relax.

"Hi Kitty," says Sergeant Evans, the gold shield who usually gets pulled into looking into Annabeth's complaints and smooths things over. His wife is one of Kitty's volunteers. He's a chubby, good-looking black guy a few years older than me, and he gives us an apologetic look. "We, uh, had a series of call-ins about you having a lot of people over."

Kitty gets it too. "Annabeth?"

Evans's partner Thompson is a big blond, almost as big as me, with a mustache that a cowboy would be proud of and a solemn manner. "Fifteen times, ma'am."

"Okay, well, come on in out of the cold and we'll sort this out." There's a faint rustle among my guys, but her calm manner, my own, and the cops' apologies do a lot to ease everyone's minds. Kitty lets them in and putters around getting them coffee, pausing to ask, "So what is she worried that I'm doing over here?"

"She noticed a line out your door this afternoon, and the entire motorcycle club parked over here, and became convinced that you were selling contraband. Her exact word is 'drugs' but I know you all don't mess with anything outside your legal grow. That was the deal when we backed the Ravens setting up over here." Evans takes his mug of coffee with a nod and a smile. "Thanks. Anyway, we promised we would check it out and make sure nothing illegal was happening."

THOMPSON'S HEAD turns as he hears a lot of mewing. "I'm detecting suspicious activity in these visitation rooms, Ev. I'm gonna go check it out."

MY DAD STARTS COUGHING into his fist, and a couple of the guys fight smirks as the big blond cop goes up to the first room's transparent door and peers in...and then immediately crouches down. His solemn expression doesn't waver.

EVANS FIGHTS a smile and coughs once. "Heh. Uh. Anyway, what was actually going on this afternoon?"

KITTY SMILES, and the whole story comes tumbling out her adorable mouth. The early spring, her asking the Ravens to help rescue a bunch of autumn litters and their families, Annabeth being more confused than usual and trying to adopt a sneaky coyote. There was more coughing and harrumphing and teary eyes at that, even from the cops.

SHE GOES on about how we're trying to get all the cats homes before winter is over, and that the first bunch got sent home today. The adopting families had their extended families, friends, and neighbors around for the holidays...and so forty-three people had come through the shelter doors.

SHE LEAVES OUT THE CRASH, the blackout, and us falling for each other and fucking like bunnies. After explaining everything else, she says simply, "Look, I think I know how to settle Annabeth's mind. Can you get her to come in here and be a witness to your investigation?" She looks at Evans—Thompson is halfway into a kitten room and being attacked by snuggling balls of fur—and he looks thoughtful.

"YEAH, I think I can arrange that. Just—" he looks back at his partner, and his belly shakes a bit with amusement. "Give me five minutes."

"WHAT HAVE you got in mind, baby?" I ask as Kitty walks back toward the kitten rooms.

"WELL, everyone's passed quarantine and is immunized, and the big crowd's gone except for you guys, who know to shut the outer door." She starts opening all the doors. Kittens and cats come spilling out into the main room, meowing and looking around, a few going hopefully for the food bowls. "You good in there, Sergeant?" she asks Thompson, who is now seated on the floor in one room's doorway with a pair of stripy kittens on his lap.

. . .

"We're A-OK," comes the solemn reply, accompanied by mewing.

"This is the cutest fuckin' thing I've ever seen," Dad chuckles, his eyes dancing. Hellcat is investigating his lap, having tired of my shoulder with all my walking around.

"Give it five minutes," Kitty replies cheerily as she tops up the fountains and food bowls.

It's not even three minutes when we hear a pair of familiar voices approaching the door outside. "No, it's not dangerous. There are no violent offenders in that building, ma'am. I've checked the Ravens' records myself."

"You mean...Kitty was telling the truth about that?" Annabeth sounds incredulous.

"Yes ma'am."

Kitty moves over to me and slips my hand into hers. It's a first in front of the family, and my Dad glances our way—but his smile just widens a little before he looks back to the door.

"Well, I know something illegal has to be going on, and I'm coming in with you with my camera to capture this for posterity. Kitty's such a nice girl. They must be manipulating her, or forcing her somehow, but they're using their land for something unspeakable!"

More choking and snorting; I press my lips together against laughter. The doorknob turns, and we all do our best to calm down.

"Well, ma'am, I will tell you that what the folks you saw coming here to pick up is pretty popular. Might even be a little addictive. But I wouldn't call it illegal or dangerous. Unless you're a canary." Evans pushes open the door and lets Annabeth in.

She's still chattering as she comes through the door, camera plastered to her determined little face as she aims it around accusingly at everything in sight. "I have no idea what you're talking about. Kitty said that she had a lot of kittens to take care of and needed the Ravens for help, but how many kittens could she possibly be—"

Her camera sweeps across the floor and takes in dozens of furry upturned faces. "Oh my God!" Her voice breaks into a squeak, like an over-excited kid's. "Oh my God, there are so many babies!"

I laugh and squeeze Kitty's hand as I look down at her. We're both relaxing as we watch Annabeth confront the most adorable cluebat to ever exist. She's already on the floor, camera still running, while trying to coax a few onto her lap with her free hand.

"Oh my goodness!" Annabeth's still squeaking, as Kitty's shoulders start to shake with suppressed laughter from watching her reaction. "Oh my goodness, I've never been so glad to be wrong in my life!"

"So glad she figured that out," Kitty says quietly, and I kiss the top of her head. People are going to start noticing that we're together, but I'm okay with that too. If Annabeth's no longer freaking out, the pressure to sneak around is gone.

It's a nice Christmas present. Not as nice as being with Kitty in the first place, but people can get two gifts in one season and appreciate them both.

Thompson reappears with a pair of stripy orange brothers in his hands, one seated in each palm with room to spare. "Yes ma'am. I think we're just glad to clear the air a little, so everyone around here can have a quiet holiday."

Evans eyes him. "You know, I was the one who went back out in the cold and negotiated this while you were off duty playing with kittens."

"I was on duty," Thompson replies placidly. Nearby, Dad's approaching the weepy-eyed Annabeth with a box of tissues and a jingly ball. *Well he doesn't waste any time.* I smile, glad he's taken his odd courtship out of my damn bushes.

Evans drains his coffee. "How do you figure?"

"Dad duty," the big blond rumbles. "I told Cara that if she turned in every homework assignment for six months, we could revisit the whole getting a kitten idea. She did it and brought up her math mark a whole grade."

Evans' eyebrows go up and he nods.

Kitty smiles up at the big cop. "So...two kittens, then?"

"A deal's a deal," comes the solemn reply.

I chuckle and shake my head, glancing over at Dad to check his progress with Annabeth. They're chatting, and he's showing off one of Hellcat's tiny kittens.

It's weird to be hanging out with cops and Annabeth, along with Dad and the boys, everyone playing with kittens and talking about normal things. But it is so much better than having the police, and that vigilante in pink, trying to get dirt on us.

. . .

AND EVEN IF it wasn't...I've got something that makes up for all the trouble. Today I woke up with my sweet Kitty next to me, and tonight I'll fall asleep with her in my arms. And I know we'll both fight like hell to make sure it stays that way from now on.

THE END.

SIGN UP TO RECEIVE FREE BOOKS

Sign Up to Receive Free E-Books and Audiobook Codes.

Would you like to read **The Unexpected Nanny, Dirty Little Virgin** and **other romance books** for **free**?

You can sign up to receive these free e-books and audiobooks by typing this link into your browser:

https://www.steamyromance.info/free-books-and-audiobooks-hot-and-steamy/

Or this one:

. . .

HTTPS://WWW.STEAMYROMANCE.INFO/THE-UNEXPECTED-NANNY-FREE/

PREVIEW OF THE HUNTER'S TREASURE

A Bad Boy MC Romance
By Lily Diamond

Blurb

Amanda

When I stepped into the abandoned Grace Memorial Hospital on Halloween night, meeting a hot guy was the last thing on my mind. I'm here for two reasons: to get over my bumbling ex-boyfriend and ex-cameraman Chad; and to create a new blockbuster video to upload to my ghost-hunting YouTube channel. Instead, just as things are getting good, I have to chase off Chad before he can sabotage my show. And then, out of nowhere, this hot guy practically falls into my lap.

Drake says he's a scout for an urban exploration team. He seems a little green, but that's all right—after fourteen episodes shot around Grace Memorial, I know this whole place's layout like no one else. I'm enjoying the company...a lot. He's smart, attractive, knows how to flirt, and makes me feel better than I ever did around Chad. Yeah, it's a little weird meeting a potential lover in a haunted hospital, but no weirder than the rest of my night. Maybe he'll be interested in giving me a happy ending to the evening....

Drake

I didn't come to the abandoned hospital where my crew and I stashed two million dollars worth of diamonds to spend the night flirting with a hot young cutie-pie. But here we are. I really like Amanda, and I feel bad about lying to her. But if I can distract her long enough to grab the diamonds, it'll be time well spent. If I'm very lucky, I'll end the night in her bed, too.

There's just one problem. My second-in-command has decided it's his time to take over the crew, and he's come with his brother to hunt me through this maze-like complex. Yes, I've got a guide; but since they captured Amanda's old cameraman, Chad, so do they. And unlike me, they have working guns. The world's hottest ghost hunter and I will have to combine our wits, skills, and resources, and figure out how to trust each other. Otherwise the hot ending to Halloween night that we're both gunning for will turn into a bloody ending instead.

CHAPTER ONE

Amanda

"This is Amanda Moss with Moss Paranormal, coming to you from Grace Memorial Hospital in Atlanta, Georgia. This is the fifteenth episode in my series on the hospital, which was abandoned twenty years ago after a series of tragic events that I cover in the series introduction. Check the link below if you're new to the series or would like a refresher."

I beam for the camera as I hold it at arm's length, still getting used to recording myself with the new rig. But since I fired Chad as both my cameraman and my boyfriend a month ago, I'm stuck handling the whole job by myself. I'll manage; I always did most of the work even when he was around.

"So anyway, guys, I know I'm way late in pushing out this episode. Thank you so much for staying loyal. I've barely lost any followers since this delay started, and as a lot of you already know, things have been pretty crazy in my personal life."

I give the camera an awkward, ironic look before letting the smile bloom again, letting my viewers know that I'm unsinkable.

Sometimes I don't really feel that way, but faking it helps me actually bounce back.

"So, now I'm back to the series—and I promise you, tonight's Halloween special is guaranteed to be worth the wait." I wink for the camera. After doing this series for so long, I know exactly how to ham it up for the camera. My little smile is conspiratorial for those who don't like girls, and just a touch flirty for those who do.

I have to be on point tonight. This is my big comeback. I've dressed the part, too—new jeans, my 18-hole Doc Martens, a plum-colored, long-sleeved t-shirt with enough v-neck to show off my ample cleavage, and my leather vest with its reflective ghost hunter patches.

My auburn hair is pulled back into a loose, thick braid. My makeup is heavier on the Goth than usual, with kohl around my green eyes and dark red lipstick. I have my usual big bag of ghost hunting gear slung over one shoulder as I walk and record.

The show must go on. Even if I've barely gotten out of my post-breakup depression. I'm doing this multi-part Halloween special for my hundreds of thousands of viewers online who support me and help me live my dream of chasing ghosts.

I don't particularly like doing it alone, but that's loneliness. Not fear. I don't miss Chad, but I miss company—and someone to hold my camera.

Chad was pretty good at the job and took direction easily, and despite being dumber than a doornail, he has a good memory—which can come in handy in this business. But he's also one of those guys who tries to fuck every single woman he runs in to. Six months ago, he weaseled his way into my pants and my wallet using a lot of emotional manipulation. I'm not dumb, but I'm kind of inexperienced with relationships, so I didn't know what warning signs to look for.

Now I do. I wish I could have learned some other way.

Chad didn't take me for much money, though he did end up living on my couch for a few months. Then he decided that because I have a big heart and trust easily, that I must be an idiot like him as well. But I had already started seeing warning signs even a newbie like me couldn't ignore.

After Chad fucked my roommate and I caught them both, I went through all the stages of grief in about a week. I took back everything the two of them had borrowed, got my name off the lease, took my stuff and moved into a cute one-bedroom across town. When Chad planted himself in my car and refused to leave until I took him to "our" new home, I threw him out and left.

After that he cried to my voicemail until I blocked him. Not even a week later, his new girlfriend called me to cuss me out about how much I had hurt him and tell me what a bitch I was being. She lasted another week before he slept with somebody else, and she called me again—to apologize this time.

I forgave her. He had manipulated me too. Softboys are the worst.

Chad—that little shit—next tried filing DMCA claims for ownership rights to the channel because of his work as my cameraman, ultimately trying to get it shut down. But poor wording and zero follow-up from his listless stoner ass meant I ended up keeping everything.

And now, finally, I'm back. New special, new gear, new filming format so I can do everything solo. Unsinkable. *Fuck you, Chad.*

I'm proud of my video channel. I've been running it since I was sixteen. For almost five solid years I've been doing urban exploration with ghost hunting videos, EVP recordings, and a book with sales that, some months, started paying my rent by itself. I did it alone at first, then with Chad for eighteen months, and now by myself again.

In the meantime, I've graduated from making recordings on my phone to using a high-quality video camera. Tonight I've brought two cameras, my phone, tripods, a separate voice recorder, and my real baby: a FLIR thermographic camera. No longer do I have to explain cold spots with just the readings on my thermometer gun. I can now *show* my viewers the cold spots and other weird temperature fluctuations associated with hauntings.

When your medium is video, visual proof is always best.

I shoot some footage of the front entrance of the hospital which has that air of genteel spookiness that all old structures in the South get eventually. It's five stories tall and three basements deep; a logic-defying maze of additions, subdivisions, retrofits and repairs. But you can't tell just how bad it is from the front facade.

I speak conversationally to the camera with the stone front gate in the foreground as I head along the tall, black iron fence toward it. "The hospital hasn't changed a bit since the last time I was here. Aside from some basic groundskeeping and a security guard, this property is pretty much abandoned. Bad for curb appeal. Good," I undo the big padlock on the gate, which has a broken hasp and opens with a tug, "for us."

It's a little white lie; I have standing permission from the property owner to shoot my program on the site. I always get permission; I even explain that in my book and one of my videos. But a little touch of rebellion and risk draws more viewers.

I swing the gate wide and it lets out a dramatic groan as I sweep the camera over to shoot the hospital's main building against the darkening sky. It's a perfect shot for my title lettering and channel info.

Great opener. You are officially back in the saddle, Mandie, my girl.

I narrate as I move slowly up the front walk, which is overshadowed by weeping willows. "On October 28, 1987, immediately before the hospital closed for good, the mental health ward became the site of a brutal spree killing. Daniel Lee Carlisle, a patient admitted for depression three months prior and with no criminal record or history of violence at all, suddenly snapped."

I walk around the corner of the building and pan the camera up to a third-floor window. The glass is shattered, and the heavy iron grating has been pushed outward so hard that it is bent and the two top bolts have been ripped from the stonework. It sticks out at an awkward angle, serving as a perch for a couple of tiny gray birds.

"Carlisle, a religious fanatic who had been rescued as a child from an extremist cult, had believed for years that he was under what he termed 'demonic oppression.' He described nightmares, visitations from shadowy figures, and an increasing feeling of doom. Two days before he was scheduled for release to a halfway house, his rampage began."

"You can see the window through which Carlisle pushed a two-hundred-and-fifty-pound metal desk with enough force to shatter the glass, bend the metal bars, and send nurse Wendy Olsen to the emergency room with a broken femur. Witnesses stated that besides displaying superhuman strength, Carlisle shouted at them in an unknown language and claimed to know what the staff and his fellow patients were thinking."

I pan down to the front steps again as I start walking up them. "Carlisle—or whatever inhabited him—took advantage of a blackout that struck the facility during a severe thunderstorm. He strangled three restrained patients to death, and beat an orderly with a chair leg before the rest of the staff managed to restrain him. It took a near overdose of sedatives to end his violence."

"Despite the staff following all possible procedures to contain the threat, and the fact that he had only sustained bruising to his face and arms, Carlisle would not last the night. Near dawn, while still safely sedated in his restraints, he suffered a massive heart attack and died in less than five minutes."

I pan back down to the ground level and walk around to the front entrance. I keep my voice as grave as possible. "According to photos of his official autopsy, his entire neck was covered in red finger marks, and he had burst blood vessels in his eyes, making it appear as though he had been strangled, despite the heart attack. The police investigated the remaining staff, but none had hands large enough to match the bruises."

It takes a hard shove to get the door open after months of rain. The heavy metal hinges screech, and I put my shoulder against the oak and shove again. The door swings aside, revealing a great shot of the dark and cavernous entry beyond.

"To this day, no one can explain Carlisle's sudden attack. Four people died that day and two more were badly injured. Was a demon involved? You be the judge."

"I'm going to play a clip for you now of Carlisle's attack immediately before the lights went out. Security cameras captured about three minutes of violence before everything suddenly went black." I walk inside as I talk, planning to use the transition into the semi-dark as the transition to the shocking footage. Then I stop, and let things run for a few seconds as I glance around.

There really hasn't been anyone in here since the last time I came by. I remember it with painful clarity—Chad got high as balls before the shoot. I spent the better part of the night trying to get halfway decent shots out of him, and ended up using the tripod most of the time because he was so useless.

Once the introduction has been filmed, I hurry back out to my battered subcompact for the duffel with my pad, food, water, sleeping bag, and a change of clothes. If it weren't for all the ghost-hunting gear, it would look like I could be doing an ordinary campout.

I double check that my car's locked up and the alarm is set before I go back inside. This isn't the best area of Atlanta, and I don't feel like taking any chances at all. I've had a good amount of success so far, but not enough that I can replace a whole car.

Once I'm back in and the duffel is tucked out of sight, I grab the camera and start back in with my backstory as I walk down the hall toward the old ER facility. "Carlisle was brought down here to the emergency room, where his bloody clothes were removed. Underneath, he was covered in long, fresh scratches."

I step through the door of the emergency room. It's one of the creepiest sections, outside of the mental hospital itself. Ragged curtains hanging in front of every alcove, the dusty nurses' counters, a crash cart lying on its side just under one of the curtains.

I sweep the camera around slowly, settling on details just long enough to make them look like they're leaping out of the shadows at viewers. "Emergency room staff labored over Carlisle and the two injured staff members whose wounds were not life threatening. Both were sent home within a few days, one of them on crutches. But Carlisle would never leave this emergency room alive."

I'm walking as I talk, and at the end of my sentence I step into one of the empty booths and let the camera's vision settle on the gurney dominating the small space.

It *moves*.

I let out a disbelieving squeak and leap back, only to laugh a little. I've somehow managed to keep my camera on the gurney as it rolls to a stop almost instantly, leaving six-inch-long streaks in the dust behind its wheels. "Oh wow. Did you guys see that? This is promising to be our best show yet!"

Little things can be just as scary as big ones when there's no ready explanation, and I'm pretty spooked myself. I put my hand over my heart and catch my breath before lifting my chin and smiling for the camera again.

"Tonight, I will be covering both the emergency room and the site of Carlisle's rampage using both EVP audio recording and a continuous video feed. In addition, I now have this." Grinning, I heft the FLIR camera.

"This is the infrared camera I was talking about in my last video! Tonight, I'm going to fire this baby up and give you a look at what was left behind in the aftermath of one of the most frightening incidents in Atlanta's paranormal history!"

I wink at the camera. "Stick around. I'm sure that this night will have a whole lot of surprises in store for all of us!"

CHAPTER TWO

Drake

The motorcycle roars under me as I open the throttle up. It's a cool, crisp Atlanta night, and the highway into town is almost clear. The chance for a burst of speed does me good; it reminds me that I am free.

I'm dressed like any late-twenties guy you'd expect to find on a motorcycle—head to toe black leather, boots, gloves, jeans, and an unmarked jacket. I'm not flying our club colors tonight. I'm flying under the radar.

I told the boys to stay back in Baton Rouge where we've got a secure hideout and plenty of money and pot. They need a break after six heists in a row, jumping from city to city to intercept jewel shipments and steal from collections. If we push too far and too hard, especially right now, we're more likely to make a mistake that will cost us.

I don't go for reckless excess. Neither does my team. We're subtle, careful, and thanks to me, we always go in disguised and knowing exactly what part each of us will play. Zero casualties, zero arrests, zero betrayals. That's the tight ship I have always kept.

Between heists, our usual cover is a small motorcycle club, perpetually "just passing through," calling ourselves the Wanderers. Friendly, selling a little pot for travel money, not asking for trouble from anyone—especially other clubs. On the roads, especially in spring and summer, we can pass for any such group of nomads.

It's all a means to an end. I play any role that's going to get us the money, freedom, and security that we need. Drunk tourist, cat burglar, parkourist, biker, cutter and setter of fake gems, cruise passenger, and just recently, jailbird.

We've gotten our routine down to the point where it's comfortable and easy to follow. After a jewel theft, we stash whatever it is we stole, grab our ready cash, and move on to the next town. We wait for things to cool down—usually six months or so—and then circle back to the cities where we have our stashes and commit no crimes at all while we retrieve them. Outside of a little trespassing, of course.

Six months on, five months off, and we leave one stash every year squirreled away long term in case something goes wrong. We end up fencing bits as we go, but keep the really choice stuff for a black market gem sale in Rio that happens every January.

Five years in a row, we have gone down the coast on an enormous cruise ship, pretending to be five brothers on our annual vacation together. Our stopover in Rio is three days, and we arrive with gems sewn into the linings of our luggage and our outer clothes. On the way back, those seams are stuffed with cash.

It's a good life, and we make bank. And for the most part, outside of a punched-out guard or something like that, we do it without any violence at all. It's so much better than what the boys and I left behind that maybe I've gotten a little complacent while I enjoyed my new life.

Maybe that's how I got caught—either that or someone didn't drop the damn dime on me. I don't know. I may never know. But I can't help but feel like I slipped up somehow.

They were waiting for us when I got back to New Orleans. I barely got to check on my houseboat before the goddamned cops were all over me. They had popped me on a gun charge for a weapon I had never seen before in my life, but had supposedly been found back in my stateroom by the maid.

I went without a fight so everyone else could take the chance to get away. Everyone else in our club has no record at all; I snapped them up before they could get into the sort of low-level crap that gets kids into trouble. I was the one the cops had something on, so I took a dive. One for all.

Maybe I'm dumb and sentimental, but after ending up in juvie for stealing to survive, I couldn't risk my boys going down too. I just don't see imprisonment as anything but hell on earth. There's no rehabilitation behind bars; just a cage you share with monsters.

I was jailed for five-and-a-half months for a crime I did not commit before they finally figured out that I was telling the truth. I could have copped a plea, but that would have meant probation, which would have thrown a giant monkey wrench into our business. And I've got my pride; if they had caught me for something I had actually done, that would be one thing, but I'm not going down for something I'm innocent of.

I was as shocked as anyone to find out about that gun; I hate the damn things. I only carry a firearm on the job or when we're playing outlaw biker out on the roads. Tonight, Max, my second-in-command, pretty much had to push a pistol at me and make me promise to take it along.

I'm an ex street kid with a lot of dumb mistakes under my

belt, but compared to the guys I met in prison, I'm a model citizen. I steal and smuggle jewels from people so rich that they will barely miss them, and I sell a little pot between gigs. I've never bullied anyone, I've never started a fight, and I've never had to use my gun.

When I think about my time in jail, those six months have a weird, dreamlike quality. I had no control of my life then—someone else told me when I could eat, sleep, exercise, everything. Once they found out I was a black belt, the gangsters and crazies mostly left me alone, but I never entirely felt safe, stable, or...real...while under those bright prison lights.

The first thing I wanted when I got out was a long motorcycle ride. So I asked the boys, since I didn't want them to see me struggling through my post-jail recovery, if I could go pick up our latest stash of diamonds by myself. That's what puts me on the highway toward Atlanta at eight on Halloween night.

I like Halloween. It's one of the most benign holidays ever. Raucous parties aside, it's pretty much all for the kids—running around playing pretend for payment in candy. It's nostalgic and silly, and when you find yourself passing those happy, noisy gaggles of small figures in costume, it can lighten the worst mood.

Once I'm off the highway I buy two shopping bags worth of full-sized chocolate bars and start tossing them to kids as I roll past—without taking my helmet off. "Thanks, Ghost Rider!" one of them yells, and I wave. I feel something relax inside of me that hasn't relented since my cell door slammed on me for the first time.

*We're pretty much rich by now. I might want to retire soon. Maybe go full normal—wife, kids. I love kids, and as for women...*I let out a chuckle as I give out the last of the chocolate bars and head to a late supper at the nearest steak place.

I've been in a cage for six months, constantly watched,

constantly...pent up. I need to get laid so badly that my balls ache sometimes, like they're over-full. I know nothing is going to really help me but a good, long fuck with a really enthusiastic woman.

But before I do that, I have a stopover to make, and then a job to do.

I park the bike and jump off as a pair of college girls are walking past toward the restaurant. I hear one of them gasp as I pull off my helmet, and can't help but smile a little. My hair is bright, white gold, and stands up in spikes just out of the helmet, so I have to smooth it down with a hand.

After months of canteen food, this is my first real meal that hasn't been delivered by a pizza guy since I got out. I order the biggest steak on their menu with all the fixings, and take over an hour downing the whole damn thing with good beer. My mood keeps improving; eventually, once I have a full belly and a little buzz, I start planning the night's short but very important job.

We stashed the jewels in an abandoned hospital called Grace Memorial. Eight months ago, before we left for Rio, I personally hid over two million dollars in unset diamonds under the floorboards of a room in their mental health wing. I'm the only one who knows exactly where they are, so it made sense to just let me go.

I scouted the place for over a week before choosing it as our stash site. There's one security guard, but the man's fifty and struggling to cover four acres of forested land on foot, on top of the building itself. As far as I know, all he does is check the doors for signs of tampering.

It's an easy job. The building's a maze inside, but the room I'm going to has a missing window with a broken metal grating. The angle of the grating and the two remaining bolts provide a convenient way for an athletic guy with the right training to get straight to that room.

My mood continues to lift as I ride over to the hospital grounds. I find myself humming—something I haven't done since I was locked up. I might be contemplating retirement after another year or so of this, but it still feels good to be getting back to what I do best.

I feel the first little hint of doubt as I see a battered little blue car sitting at the curb immediately outside the front gates. It could be the security guy's, but he usually parks in the back as far as I know. Its presence sets my nerves on edge. Is someone else here?

A fat, drooping live oak sits at the property line near the gate. I park in its shadow, secure my bike, grab my backpack with my minimal gear and strap it on. Then, after a glance around to make sure I'm not being followed, I scramble right up the tree trunk and swing over the iron fence on a sturdy branch.

I land in a crouch, glancing around again. I still have my helmet on since I want my head protected if I have to do some climbing—and my face covered in case I actually do run into anyone. I'm pretty distinctive—I've always been a big guy, and I got even more into bodybuilding while I was inside. But the helmet makes me anonymous enough.

I still can't get used to the idea that I can see the sky as much as I want. I still can't get used to the idea that I can go pretty much wherever I want, whenever—as long as I take precautions not to get caught. My false imprisonment has left me with a greater appreciation for freedom than ever before.

Now let's not fuck it up.

I approach the building cautiously, staying in the shadows. Down the hill from me, a flashlight bobs as the security guy doggedly makes his usual rounds. I don't have to worry about him. But I need to get past the tree line so I can get a good view of that hospital wing.

Finally, I reach the knot of trees closest to that side of the building and peer up at the window where I'm supposed to make my entrance...

Only to see a light shining in it.

Fuck, I think, as I stare up at the lit window in this supposedly abandoned building. *Who is this now? Are they looking for the diamonds? If they're here for some other reason, is it possible that they'll stumble onto them?*

I can't just leave and take the chance that the diamonds are safe. I have to check this out—and pray that I can still retrieve them without risking being seen.

Muttering in irritation, I head for the entrance, planning to slip inside and quietly investigate this unexpected intruder.

If you want to continue reading this story, you can get your copy from your favorite vendor by searching for the title:

The Hunter's Treasure
A Bad Boy MC Romance

You can also find the e-book version by typing this link in your computer's browser:

https://www.hotandsteamyromance.com/products/the-hunter-s-treasure-a-bad-boy-mc-romance

OTHER BOOKS BY THIS AUTHOR

Saving Her Rescuer: A Billionaire & A Virgin Romance

I was just trying to get away from my crazy ex for the weekend when I ended up in a giant pileup on the highway up to Gore Mountain.

https://geni.us/SavingHerRescuer

∽

Sensual Sounds: A Rockstar Ménage

Lust. Lies. Double lives.

The rock and roll industry is full of people who are looking out for themselves and willing to do anything to rise to the top.

https://www.hotandsteamyromance.com/collections/frontpage/products/sensual-sounds-a-rockstar-menage

On the Run: A Secret Baby Romance

Murder. Lies. Fraud. Just another day in the lives of billionaires and women on the run.

https://www.hotandsteamyromance.com/collections/frontpage/products/on-the-run-a-secret-baby-romance

The Dirty Doctor's Touch: A Billionaire Doctor Romance

I am a master. An elitist. I am at the top of my field, and I know what I am doing.

https://www.hotandsteamyromance.com/collections/frontpage/products/the-dirty-doctor-s-touch-a-billionaire-doctor-romance

The Hero She Needs: A Single Daddy Next Door Romance

He's the only man I've ever wanted...

https://www.hotandsteamyromance.com/collections/frontpage/products/the-hero-she-needs-a-single-daddy-next-door-romance

Other Books By This Author

You can find all of my books here:

Hot and Steamy Romance
    https://www.hotandsteamyromance.com

©Copyright 2020 by Lily Diamond - All rights Reserved
In no way is it legal to reproduce, duplicate, or transmit any part of this document in either electronic means or in printed format. Recording of this publication is strictly prohibited and any storage of this document is not allowed unless with written permission from the publisher. All rights are reserved.
Respective authors own all copyrights not held by the publisher.

 Created with Vellum

www.ingramcontent.com/pod-product-compliance
Lightning Source LLC
LaVergne TN
LVHW011730060526
838200LV00051B/3109